My Big
Bedtime Book of
MAKE-BELIEVE

illustrated by Jane Launchbury

AWARD PUBLICATIONS LIMITED

ISBN 0-86163-867-0

Copyright © 1987 Templar Publishing

First published 1987 by Century Hutchinson Children's Books

This edition first published 1996

Published by Award Publications Limited,
27 Longford Street, London NW1 3DZ

Printed in Spain

CONTENTS

DAVID
AND
THE DRAGON

by Jane Launchbury

There was a cold north wind blowing as David started the long walk home from school. The little boy shivered, and pulled the hood of his coat down over his eyes to keep out the biting cold. He walked faster when he reached the start of the woodland path, partly to keep warm, and partly because the light was beginning to fade and he hated being in the wood when it was dark. He had a very vivid imagination, and in his mind there were horrible monsters lurking behind the creaking old trees, just waiting to pounce on him. Every crack of a breaking twig made him jump and walk a little faster. He did not dare to look over his shoulder.

David hurried along the woodland path, glancing nervously into the shadows around him. He was in the thickest part of the wood, near the middle, when he saw

4

an extraordinary thing. Straight ahead of him, through the tangled brambles and briars, he caught a glimpse of sparkling colours and a puff of smoke. In the fading light he couldn't be sure, but he was convinced that there was a huge scaly monster lurking in the undergrowth. David stopped in his tracks. He would have to find a different way home. There was no way that he was going anywhere near whatever it was in the bushes.

Taking a deep breath and speeding up, David turned down a tiny path made by the woodland animals. He was almost running when he saw the thing again — in fact he very nearly tripped over it! From behind an old beech tree trailed a long spiny tail covered in glistening scales. The end of the tail reached right into the middle of the path. From the other side of the tree came little puffs of smoke. There was now no doubt in David's mind. In the middle of Oakapple Wood there was a real, live, fire-breathing dragon!

5

David gulped and gave a little squeak of fright. He tried to think what the brave knights did in all the fairy tales he knew. Somehow they always seemed to be armed with magic swords and shields. Pulling the hood of his coat even further over his eyes, David picked up a big stick. It would have to do instead of a magic sword. Then he thought that perhaps if he crept past the tree very quietly, the dragon might not notice him. But just as he started to move, he tripped over his shoelace and trod heavily on the scaly tail. There was a loud yelp of pain from behind the tree.

David started to shiver all over, and his teeth began to chatter. He was rooted to the spot with terror. Then above the sound of his own teeth chattering, he heard another sound. Someone else's teeth were chattering too.

"Whoever it is must have lots of teeth," thought David. Then, out of the corner of his eye, he saw something appear round the edge of the beech tree. It was the end of a thin green and yellow snout and there were little plumes of smoke rising from its nostrils.

David pulled the edges of his hood so tightly together that he could only peep out through a tiny crack.

He watched with terrified fascination as more of the snout appeared. The noise of chattering teeth got louder. David gasped in surprise as he realised what that meant – the dragon was just as frightened as he was. All its teeth were chattering, and there must have been at least a hundred of them! Then a pair of very frightened orange eyes peeped around the edge of the tree.

David opened the crack in his hood a little wider, and for a long time he and the dragon looked at each other nervously. Gradually their teeth stopped chattering, although the dragon was still shivering gently. Very slowly, David pushed back the hood of his coat and smiled shyly at the dragon. It grinned in the best way that a dragon can, and David gave a little giggle. Instead of the great sharp teeth he had been expecting, the dragon had tiny rounded teeth like shiny white pearls. It was still very young and hadn't got its proper teeth yet.

7

Very slowly, so as not to frighten the boy, the young dragon crept out from behind the tree. It had short stumpy legs, with great big feet, and down its back were soft leathery spines. Tufts of ginger hair grew out of its two huge green ears which seemed several sizes too big. All over the dragon's body were shiny scales, glistening in the colours of the rainbow. A gust of icy wind blew through the trees, and David realised that the poor little dragon was cold! He took off his coat and put it over the creature's back.

"Thank you," whispered the dragon.

Then it took a deep breath and told David all about itself. It wasn't a very long story. The dragon's name was Jamie, and he had been born very late in the summer, up in the mountains to the north. Normally when autumn came, all the dragons migrated south, flying to warmer places for the winter. But, because Jamie was so small, he didn't have the strength to fly with all the others and had been left behind in the cold. He had flown as far as the wood and then run out of energy. A little tear ran down Jamie's scaly cheek as he told David how cold and frightened he had been in the wood.

David knew just how the dragon felt. He also knew

how to help Jamie. His mother's tiny cottage was only a few minutes away. Inside, the dragon would be cosy and warm. It was the only place to be on a cold, dark night like this. David's mother had a kind heart, and loved all the woodland animals. He was sure that she would take pity on the little creature.

David led the small, shivering dragon through the wood. As they came in sight of his home, Jamie already looked a great deal happier. David's mother was enchanted with the dragon, who was very polite and well mannered. She let him curl up in the best chair in front of the fire, and busied herself making a pot of rich, creamy soup and special biscuits.

The days went by, and Jamie lost his bewildered, sad look and began to get stronger. He stayed with David and his mother throughout that long, cold winter, and every night he told them a different story — for dragons have very vivid imaginations and are wonderful storytellers.

Spring came and the evenings got lighter. Jamie sat outside the cottage, looking up into the sky. Then one day the dragon saw what he had been waiting for – his family were heading back to the mountains for the summer. Cheerfully, he unfurled his wings, and with whoops of delight, rose gracefully into the sky. Then all the dragons swooped low over the tiny cottage calling out their thanks to David and his mother before heading off to their summer home in the mountains.

For many years afterwards David watched the skies for the migrating dragons every time that spring arrived, but he never saw any of them again. Though sometimes he fancied that he could hear their gentle voices calling "Hello" on the wind that blew down from the mountains. Then he realised just how lucky he was to have met a real, live dragon as nice as Jamie had been – for, after all, not many people do these days, do they?

THE END

11

PRINCE FANSHAW'S SPECIAL MONSTER

by Deborah Tyler

Once upon a time, for that is how all proper fairy stories begin, there was a prince. His name was Prince Fanshaw and his parents, Queen Matilda and King Bruno the Wonderful, ruled over the land of Mordinia. They were happy, but they had a problem – the Prince would not marry! They had given hundreds of balls, concerts and parties in his honour. Yet he had not asked a single girl to dance.

"They are so dull," complained the Prince. "I don't like any of them and I *certainly* wouldn't marry them."

"But all princes get married," said King Bruno. "It is their royal duty." So King Bruno arranged that his son should start rescuing as many fair maidens as possible in the hope he might meet one that he liked. First, Prince Fanshaw saved Princess Maribel Mont Percy from a giant toad. "BORING!" he yawned. Then he rescued Lady Eleanor De Sax from a dragon. "TEDIOUS!" he cried.

So, in the end, the King and Queen just gave up.

One day, when he had finished rescuing Lady Gillian Hope-Jones from a particularly smelly sea monster, Prince Fanshaw decided to go for a long walk. He was sick of being a hero. In fact, he wished that everyone would leave him alone. Wherever he went, the locals would shout: "Look, there's brave Prince Fanshaw!" Or, "Long live the Mordinian monster slayer!"

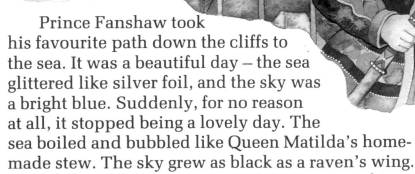

Prince Fanshaw took his favourite path down the cliffs to the sea. It was a beautiful day – the sea glittered like silver foil, and the sky was a bright blue. Suddenly, for no reason at all, it stopped being a lovely day. The sea boiled and bubbled like Queen Matilda's home-made stew. The sky grew as black as a raven's wing.

"I hope it doesn't rain," said the Prince to himself. "My sword will rust up." But it did rain, very heavily, and soon huge drops were rolling down his sword buckle.

13

Prince Fanshaw looked around him. He saw a cave cut into the rock that he had never noticed before, and he ran down the rough path towards it. It was a cave which smelt of the sea and the wind. There was a bunch of seaweed hanging above the entrance and a sign which read:

"Please knock. No Tradespeople. Wipe your feet."

So he knocked on the side of the cave.

"Who is it?" asked a soft, girlish voice. There was something sad about it, like the rustle of sea grass.

"May I come in?" asked the Prince. "It is I, Prince Fanshaw, and it's raining jolly hard."

"Oh! You are the monster slayer?" said the voice.

"Yes," replied the Prince.

"Well then, you can't come in, for I am a monster!"

"Have you eaten any fair maidens?" asked Prince Fanshaw with a sigh. The creature within gave a gasp.

"No!" it cried in horror. "You see, I once was a maiden myself!"

14

"I won't hurt you," said the Prince, "but I don't quite understand. What do you mean, you used to be a maiden?"

"You had better come in and hear my story," said the small voice. So Prince Fanshaw entered the cave. It had walls with fish painted upon them and it seemed to be empty, but the same small voice spoke again from the shadows.

"Once," it began, "I was a princess. I was the Princess Floella and I lived in a lovely white castle, with fountains and peacocks. But I was very vain and very spoiled. I would not eat anything but the best chocolates and I would only wear dresses made of silk and pearls. I was very rude to everyone, especially my mother and father – I even threw food at the princes who came to court me. Then I made my great mistake. On my sixteenth birthday, I hit the court magician with a blackcurrant pie. I had aimed it at Prince Dortimand, who was in love with me, but it hit the magician instead. He was so angry he turned me into a monster, and I was immediately banished. But now I'm really very sorry for what I did," sniffed the monster. "I am no longer spoiled."

15

Prince Fanshaw had listened to the tale in silence. Now he spoke up.

"Is there no cure?" he asked.

"I will only change back if a prince can love me and marry me as I am," replied the monster. "But what prince would marry a lizard!" And with that the creature stepped forward out of the shadows. She was indeed a lizard – a lizard with greenish-brown, slimy scales, wearing a tattered white party dress and a little gold crown. Prince Fanshaw smiled.

"Floella, you are a very special lizard," he said. Princess Floella smiled back, showing her pointed fangs. "So special that I want to marry you," said the Prince. And he took her back to the castle with him.

"Father," he said. "This is Princess Floella. I want to marry her."

The King was horrified.

"My dear boy!" he exclaimed. "You can't marry a lizard!" At this point, the Queen fainted. There was a great uproar in the court and the court lawyers were summoned, but they could find nothing which stated that it was against the law for a prince of the realm to marry a lizard if he wanted to.

No one would believe that Floella was really a princess. The ladies-in-waiting avoided her, and the Queen was very rude.

"What sort of royal wedding will this be," she cried, "with a lizard as a bride!"

Floella loved Fanshaw with all her heart. She was deeply sorry, for his sake, that she looked like a horrible monster. As a princess she had never, ever been sorry for anyone. What if she did not change back to a

16

princess after the wedding and he remained married to a lizard all his life? And the more she thought, the more she worried until, one day, she decided to run away.

On the night before her wedding, Floella packed a small bag and tried to leave the castle. As she passed the castle fountain she shed two tears. Two diamond drops rolled down her scaly skin. Suddenly, she felt herself shudder and heard a crack like glass breaking. Then she heard Prince Fanshaw's voice.

"Floella, where are you going?" he cried.

"I can't marry you," she sighed. "I love you too much to see you married to a lizard." Then she looked at the ground. There, on the floor, was her lizard skin!

"No!" Fanshaw exclaimed. "You are beautiful! Look into the fountain pool."

18

Princess Floella looked into the pool. The lizard scales had gone and a beautiful girl looked up at her. She had creamy-white skin, lovely amber eyes and a mass of dark curly hair. The only sign that she had ever been a lizard was a streak of green through one of her curls. Floella wept for joy.

The wedding of Prince Fanshaw and Princess Floella was a very merry occasion. The castle and cathedral were decorated with garlands of roses and beautiful sea shells. And the children of the land hung paper fish from all the trees. Floella and Fanshaw were very happy together. They ruled their kingdom wisely and well, and in time they had a son. He was a handsome boy with golden hair – and eyes as green as a lizard.

THE END

THE
STORM
MONSTER

by Gina Stewart

Peter lay in his bed in the little room under the eaves at the top of the house. He should have been fast asleep by now, but something had woken him up. He listened for a while and heard the sound of the waves beginning to crash and pound on the beach close to his home, and a moaning and a creaking as the tall pines in the forest swayed in the wind.

Peter's heart began to beat a little faster. He didn't know whether to feel excited or scared, but he knew for certain that somewhere out at sea a tremendous storm was brewing, and that it was moving in the direction of his home.

All night the tempest raged, thundering and buffeting against the house as though it meant to tear it down stone by stone. At last, when it was almost

morning, the wind dropped, giving way to a grey,
cloudy, rainy day.

"There'll be lots of things blown in on the tide,"
said Peter at breakfast time. "*Please* may I go to the
beach and see?"

"All right, Peter," said his mother with a smile. So
Peter put on his anorak and wellington boots and ran
down the stony path to the beach.

"Wow!" he said as he reached the sand. He had
never seen the beach looking like this before. Everywhere
he looked there was driftwood and seaweed, bottles
and plastic containers, wooden planks and ... and ...
Peter couldn't believe his eyes. There, lying upside-
down near some rocks was a green wooden rowing-boat.

"Oh, thank you, storm!" said Peter. "It's just what
I've always wanted."

Peter ran across the sand towards the little boat.
He was just pulling some of the
strands of seaweed away from
the hull, when a dreadful
groan stopped him
in his tracks.

"Help!" the groan seemed to say. "Please help me!"

Peter realized that the sound was coming from underneath the boat. Although the voice was saying words that Peter understood, it wasn't like a human voice, but deep and gurgly and rather frightening. Peter was about to run back to fetch his father when the strange voice spoke again.

"Please don't go!" it said. "I can't breathe and I'm dying of thirst!"

Gathering all his strength together, Peter started tugging and heaving at the boat, but all he could do was lift one side enough to prop a small rock underneath the edge so that air could get in.

"That's ... that's a little better," gasped the voice. "Thank you ..."

"That's all right," said Peter and he knelt down by the boat and peered underneath. It took a moment for his eyes to get used to the darkness, but when they did he jumped back in terror.

For underneath the boat was a monster, a huge creature with a great round head and enormous, sad eyes.

"Please could you get me some water!" it said unhappily. "My throat's full of sand!"

Peter ran off along the beach and soon found a plastic box with rainwater in it. Carefully, he picked up the container and went back to the boat. As he passed the plastic box under the edge, two strange long arms shot out and grabbed it. There was a long gurgling noise, followed almost immediately by a violent spitting sound.

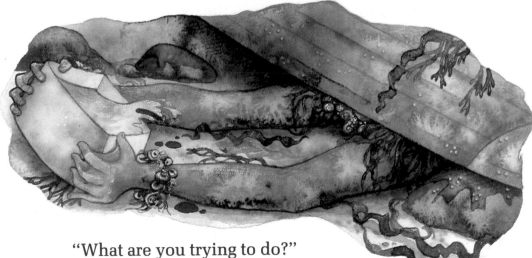

"What are you trying to do?" said the creature under the boat. "Poison me?"

"Why? What do you mean?" asked Peter.

"This is *fresh* water!" cried the monster in disgust.

"Oh, I see!" said Peter, quickly refilling the box from a nearby rock pool. "Is this what you wanted?"

While the creature drank several containers of salt water, one after the other, Peter sat and stared at it, wondering how it came to be there.

As if reading his thoughts, the monster said:

23

"My home is at the bottom of the farthest ocean, but I was caught on the surface when that terrible storm blew up last night. Of course, once I was in shallow water I couldn't swim, and then a tremendous wave swept me up to the top of the beach. And just when I thought I'd found a boat to float myself back to sea in, it toppled over on top of me. And here I am. Trapped. Normally I could shift a boat this size in a twinkling, but at the moment I feel rather weak."

"Can I get you anything to eat?" asked Peter.

"What have you got?" said the monster, quickly.

"Well ...," Peter peered into the rock pool. "There's seaweed, or limpets, or starfish, or shrimps ..."

"That'll do," said the monster.

"Which one?" asked Peter.

"All of them, of course!" said the monster hungrily. "And make sure the seaweed isn't all dry and nasty!"

It was easy catching the little creatures in the rock pool, and soon the monster was crunching away happily

"And while I'm eating," said the monster, with its mouth full, "you can think of a way to get me out of here."

"I am thinking," said Peter, "and I've got an idea. Tonight is the highest tide of the year," he went on, "and I'll be back then. But first you should have a rest and get your strength back."

Some hours later, when it was quite dark outside and his parents were fast asleep, Peter crept down the stairs of his house and ran down the rocky path to the beach.

"Hello, monster," he said as he reached the boat.

"You'll be pleased to hear," said the monster, "that I've managed to roll onto my back and I can now move my legs a little. Perhaps, together, we can move this boat."

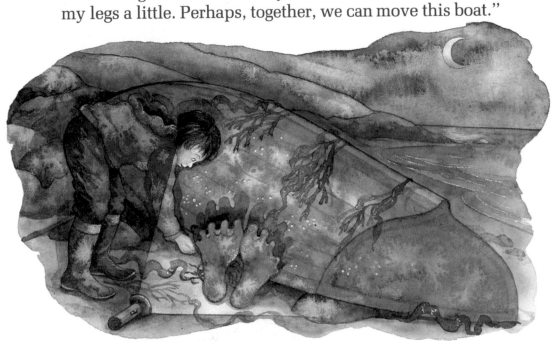

At first Peter and the monster tried to lift the boat, but nothing happened. Then on the third attempt the monster, still lying on his back, gave a mighty heave. One side of the boat rose up in the air, then wobbled a little ... and then fell right way up, with a plop, onto the sand. There before Peter stood the strangest creature he had ever seen. It was blue and green – the colour of the deepest oceans – with long hair that hung like seaweed down its back. Around its head was a crown of pearly shells, and its wrists and ankles were hung with limpets and periwinkles and tiny, shiny pebbles.

25

"Now help me get in," said the monster, clambering into the little boat. Moments later, when the water was already lapping around Peter's feet, the sea monster was safely on board.

"There aren't any oars!" cried Peter in dismay.

But it didn't matter. The monster spread its great, long arms to their full width and, as the water lifted the boat off the sand, began paddling its way out to sea.

"Thank you!" it shouted as it vanished from sight. "Thank you, my friend!"

Next morning dawned blue, sunny and still. Peter awoke feeling sad. He knew that by now the monster would have reached deep water and would have swum down to its home at the bottom of the ocean. He would never see his new friend again.

But when he went down the stony path to the beach later that day, a marvellous sight greeted him. There, tied to a rock by a piece of seaweed, was the green rowing-boat in which the monster had paddled away the night before. And inside was a brand new pair or oars!

THE END

THE LAST OF THE MONSTERS

by Philip Steele

Do you believe in monsters? There is one old gentleman who does. His name is Professor Knickerbocker, and he looks a bit like a monster himself – a friendly monster, that is. He has a thick mane of white hair, shaggy eyebrows and a long white beard. He keeps several pairs of spectacles tied around his neck with string, and he is a famous monsterologist.

One day Professor Knickerbocker announced he was going on a journey around the world.

"Is it going to be a holiday?" asked his niece Carrie. "Can I come too?"

"Oh, you can come," replied the Professor. "But you must understand that this is a *scientific* expedition. I am going to search for the Scaly Scalliwags!"

"What on earth are they?" asked Carrie.

"Monsters!" said the Professor, darkly.

"But surely monsters and dragons only exist in books?" said Carrie. But the Professor shook his head.

"Long ago," he said, "there were all kinds of monsters in the world. There was the Abominable Snowman and his relatives the Greater Hairy Bigfoot and the Lesser Spotted Yeti. Then there was the Sabre-Toothed Weevil, the dreaded Nasti-Nasti and the common or garden Wibbly-Wobbly. Today, alas, there are no monsters left — with the *possible* exception of the Scaly Scalliwag from Outer Korkovia! Some very strange footprints have been discovered in the jungle there."

"But *why* aren't there any monsters left?" asked Carrie. She knew the Professor could never resist answering a question, even if it was time for her to go to bed!

"Well my dear, that is a sad story. The monsters were harmless enough, but the trouble was that people were always picking fights with them. At one time no self-respecting princess could get married unless her young man had first killed a monster, or a giant, or a dragon. The last few monsters had to hide away in caves and lakes, and all sorts of uncomfortable places."

"Which were the *scariest* monsters?" asked Carrie.

"Hmmm... Time for bed," said the Professor. "We must pack first thing in the morning."

The very next day Carrie and Professor Knickerbocker set out for the airport. Carrie had a neat little backpack, and the Professor had an ancient suitcase tied up with straps. Sticking out of it were butterfly nets and umbrellas, tent pegs and bootlaces – and what looked like a very strange trombone! The people at the airport gave him some funny looks until they heard it was the famous Professor Knickerbocker. Then they waved him on to the plane.

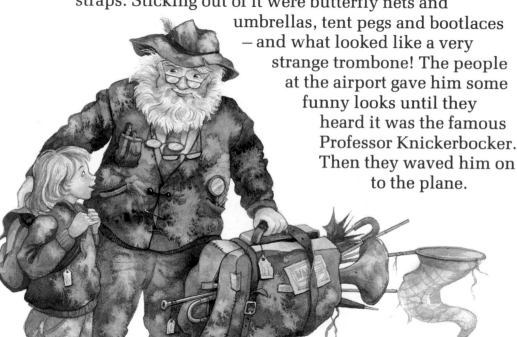

Soon the plane took off, and within eight hours they were in the tropics! They then had to go on a long train ride over the mountains, across a desert on camels and *then* up a river full of crocodiles. It took them a whole month to reach the jungles of Korkovia!

"Where are the monsters, then?" asked Carrie when they got there. She was feeling hot and bothered.

"Our search has only just begun," replied the Professor. "Deep in the jungle there is a great cliff full of deep tunnels and potholes. It is there that the footprints were seen."

So off they set through the thick, thick jungle. They passed beautiful waterfalls and swamps full of squirming snakes. At last they came to the foot of the great cliffs. Aha! There were the footprints all right! Great claw marks led across soft mud into the depths of a dark tunnel.

"I hope we haven't got to go in there," said Carrie with a shiver.

"Not if my plan works out!" said the Professor. He rummaged in his suitcase and brought out the strange-looking trombone. Raising it to his lips, he puffed out his cheeks and blew till he was red in the face.

Broop-broop-brarrrrrp! Broop-broop-braaaaarrrrp! Broop-BRAAAAAAAARRRP! The noise echoed around the cliffs. There was a moment's silence, and then a reply came from the darkest tunnel:

Broop-broop-braaaAAAARRRRRP!

Out skipped a Scaly Scalliwag, blinking in the sun. He had long woolly hair, green scaly legs and a nose shaped like a trumpet, which made the strange sound.

"A Scaly Scalliwag!" breathed the Professor. "Just fancy that!"

"You tricked me!" cried the monster. "I thought it was another scalliwag! I was *so* looking forward to a chat!"

"Good heavens!" said Professor Knickerbocker. "You understand human speech!"

"Of course I do. I learnt it at Scalliwag School, about four hundred years ago."

"My, oh my!" said the professor scribbling notes. "Now tell me, where do the other scalliwags live?"

"Other scalliwags? What other scalliwags? I am the last of my kind," said thé monster, and a large tear rolled down his cheek. "Fifty years ago I fell asleep at a party and when I woke up, the tunnel was empty. All the other scalliwags had gone. They're probably as dead as dodos, for I've never seen them again. Boo-hoo!"

"Oh, you poor old scalliwag," said Carrie. And she reached up and patted him on the back.

"Do you mind if I ask you some questions?" said the Professor briskly.

"Oh, all right, why not?" said the scalliwag. So for the rest of that day they sat there by the cliffs, while the Professor asked questions like, "Did your grandmother have orange spots?" and "What do you like for breakfast?" Soon they were all the best of friends. When it was time for them to go, the Scaly Scalliwag cleared his throat.

"Ahem...Er...Do you think I could come home with you and live in your country?"

The Professor looked at his niece, and she whispered

something. Then the Professor held out his hand.

"Scalliwag," he said, "we'll ship you home in a crate. You won't mind that, will you?"

Mind it? The Scaly Scalliwag jumped for joy.

Near Professor Knickerbocker's home in the city is the entrance to an underground railway station. One dark night in autumn he and Carrie led an excited Scaly Scalliwag down the escalator and into the tunnel. There, in a deep, dark siding, the monster happily made his home. He wasn't lonely any more. He could see trains going by and listen to the noisy crowds. Sometimes he pulled faces through the train windows, but the Professor told him to stop or he would cause an accident. He still lives down there to this day, or so I'm told.

And according to Carrie, Professor Knickerbocker just might have some good news in store for the monster. He thinks he has traced some other Scaly Scalliwags living in the Mountains of Mombo. She's keeping her fingers crossed. Are you?

THE END

A
STITCH
IN TIME

by Sue Seddon

There was once a young princess called Kate. She lived with her parents and her brothers in a beautiful, high-towered palace set on the side of a hill above a wide silver river. In the mornings, Kate learned to play music and dance in the Great Hall. In the afternoons, she went to her grandmother's private rooms, with their huge arched windows that looked down over the green palace gardens to the glittering river, and she learned to sew.

Kate's grandmother sewed the most wonderful embroideries anyone had ever seen. They were fantastic pictures in silk and wool, of flowery gardens, splendid gods and goddesses, handsome knights and extraordinary monsters. The embroideries hung all over the palace and people came from far and wide to see them. They

were so life-like that many people believed that they
must be magic.

Kate longed to sew as beautifully as her grandmother.
She had spent hours studying the embroideries – and
she had noticed a very strange thing. Her grandmother
never completely finished the figures in her embroideries.
In each case, a couple of tiny stitches were always
missing. One afternoon she decided to ask her
grandmother why she never completed her figures.

"Well, my dear child," said her grandmother,
mysteriously, "that is the magic part."

"What do you mean, Grandmother?" asked the
princess.

"Come here and I'll show you," she replied. So Kate
got up from the velvet cushion where she was sitting,
and looked down at the embroidery her grandmother
was working on.

It was a picture of Kate herself, but slightly older.
There she was, in a beautiful silk dress, with a little
crown on her golden head, standing
at the entrance to a huge dark cave.
At her side was a monster!
It had long, curved horns
like a bull, the body
of a lion and great
gold-red wings.

"Ooh, Grandmother," Kate cried. "It's a wonderful monster!" She looked closer. "I can see where you haven't finished it," she said. "Look, there are some stitches missing from its feet!"

"You have got sharp eyes," laughed her grandmother. Then she grew serious. "I have a very special reason for always leaving a little bit of the figures in my embroideries unfinished, my dear," she said. "And it is a magic reason. You see, if I did finish any of them they might become more than just embroideries!"

"You mean they would come to life?" gasped Kate.

"Well, they might," said her grandmother. She would say no more, so Kate changed the subject.

"What's going in this space?" she asked.

"Oh, that's for the prince," said her grandmother, smiling.

"Really! Is it going to be the man that I'll marry?"

"We'll see, we'll see," murmured her grandmother. But Kate knew that it was.

"I can't wait for you to finish it, so that I can see him," she said. "Please may I help you!"

"Well yes, I think you may," said the old lady. So Kate carried on sewing the brightly coloured little flowers at the feet of the monster, while her grandmother embroidered the prince.

They continued to sew together, happy in each other's company. The sun was setting over the silver river, when Kate's grandmother decided it was time to stop. She looked down to see how her granddaughter was getting on. To her horror she saw that Kate was about to sew in the very last stitch on the monster.

"No!" she cried. But it was too late. Kate had finished the stitch.

There was a great blue flash, and the embroidery was twisted out of their hands. It flew up into the air and began to spin around in the centre of the room. Faster and faster it span, like a whirlwind. Then, gradually, it began to slow down and change shape. Kate clung to her grandmother, hardly daring to look. When she did open her eyes, she gasped – there, in the centre of the room, stood the monster from the embroidery!

"Who called me?" groaned the monster sadly.

Kate found her voice. "I did," she said.

"I wish you hadn't," sighed the monster.

"Oh dear, I am sorry," whispered Kate.

"Well, please put me back immediately," he begged.

"I don't think I can," said Kate. "Why don't you stay here with me. We could have lots of adventures together."

"You don't understand," moaned the monster. "I'll die if I can't get back into the embroidery by sunrise." So saying, he leapt through the window and flew away into the dusk.

"Oh, poor monster," said Kate and started to cry.

"There is no time to waste on tears," said her grandmother. "I think we may be able to help him. But we must complete the embroidery as soon as possible. Only then can the monster return."

The embroidery was lying in a heap in the middle of the room. Kate picked it up nervously, but nothing happened. There was a space where the monster had been, but otherwise it looked just the same. Kate and her grandmother settled down to complete it. They sewed through the night. No one else could help them, as only they could break the spell. Sometimes, Kate thought she could hear the monster sighing outside the window and that made her sew even faster.

At last the prince was almost complete. Kate's grandmother gave a triumphant cry as she put in the last stitch. This time there was a bright green flash. The embroidery flew out of their hands and started to spin like a whirlwind.

40

In the centre Kate could just make out the shape of a man. It was the prince! Suddenly he was in the room with them. Kate just had time to think how handsome he was, when there was a happy roar and the monster flew back into the room. It was almost dawn now, and Kate's grandmother looked worried.

"We must hurry, my dear child," she cried. "There is the background to complete – and we must also bring the princess to life!"

It was Kate who sewed the final stitch into the princess. There was a dazzling yellow flash, and there was Kate! The two Kates smiled at each other. Then the embroidery princess joined the prince and the monster, anxiously waiting by the great windows.

Kate and her grandmother continued to sew. The sky was coloured with the first pink rays of the rising sun, when her grandmother finished the last flower. This time there were no bright flashes. Instead, there

41

was the sound of birds singing and, before their eyes, the room changed into the beautiful garden of the embroidery! Bees buzzed through brilliant red poppies and glorious butterflies hovered over twinkling streams.

"Home, sweet home," cried the monster, as he bounded into the dark cave in the centre of the flowery garden. The prince and princess waved goodbye, as they stepped into the garden after him. The next moment, the sun was streaming in through the great, arched windows – and the embroidery picture had gone!

"Now you must promise me *never* to meddle with my magic again, Kate," said her grandmother. "I will sew the picture again, and when you are a little older, I promise that I'll put the last stitch in your prince and he'll come back to marry you."

And, do you know, that's just what happened. And the monster? He remained happily in his embroidered cave for ever.

THE END

THE CIVILISED SNOWMAN

by Deborah Tyler

The magic started with the very special present Paul Plank's dad gave him one Christmas. Paul's dad was not an ordinary dad. He did not have a normal job like most other dads – for he was a famous mountain climber! It was very exciting to have a famous father, but it upset Paul at Christmas, because his dad was almost always away. Paul usually saw his dad then on the television news, wearing goggles and a woolly hat, and waving from the top of some white and glittering mountain.

Paul wished that he too could climb mountains and have adventures in a far-off, pure white world. He imagined himself there, where the sun shone down on a land of icing sugar and the flakes of snow were as soft and as large as goose feathers. He wished most of all that he could meet that strange mountain monster, the Abominable Snowman. Not even his dad had met the Abominable Snowman – although he had, one dark afternoon, seen a huge footprint in the snow. Then, one Christmas, everything changed.

On Christmas Eve, Paul's dad left home to climb the highest mountain in the world. Before setting off, he placed a large, round present, with a very solid base, on Paul's bedside table. It was wrapped in brown paper and it had a sprig of holly on the top so it looked just like a big Christmas pudding. Paul was so excited, he couldn't sleep at all. He lay in bed thinking. What could the present be?

Just as he was about to fall asleep, he noticed a strange glow had filled the room. Paul got out of bed and looked out of the window, but it was dark and rainy outside. Then he looked at his present. It seemed to be shimmering with a bright light!

Paul looked at the bedside clock. It was only eleven o'clock! But he couldn't wait any longer. Carefully, he pulled away the brown paper. There, nestled inside was a glass 'snowstorm', the kind you can shake to make the snow fall!

Paul looked at his present in amazement as it began to glow even more fiercely. Inside the crystal dome there was a snowy mountain, with a glittering ice cap. The sky behind it was purple and dotted with silver stars. And whirling round the mountain were hundreds of tiny snowflakes, like a great white blizzard. Paul looked again at his clock. It was nearly midnight. He reached out to shake the snowstorm but as soon as his hands touched the glass, the room was bathed in a blinding, white light. He could no longer feel the glass beneath his fingers and, before he knew it, he was being pulled into the snowstorm. He could feel himself whirling like the snowflakes, and feel the cold, cold mountain wind on his cheeks. Whatever was happening?

The next moment, Paul found himself sitting on the icy peak of a huge, white mountain. It was like sitting on a diamond, and it was very cold – especially as Paul was only wearing pyjamas. He looked about him. Down below there were probably pine forests and wolves. Up here, everything was white and silent. Then he heard singing! Someone very near was happily singing away in a rich, deep voice. The song ended with a couple of "Pom-tiddley-poms".

Just then the singer stepped out from behind an icy peak. It was a monster! It was not an ugly monster, but it certainly looked very odd. It was covered from head to foot in soft, white fur and had long ears which hung down like a spaniel's. The monster had large, brown eyes and a great bush of fur under its nose, which looked rather like a huge moustache. It reminded Paul of his great-uncle Edwin, the famous climber, whose pictures he had seen in the Museum of Mountaineering. Great-uncle Edwin had got lost on a climbing expedition and had never been seen again.

"I say," said the monster. "A visitor!" Paul smiled.

"Hello," he said. "Are you the Abominable Snowman?"

The monster roared irritably. Then he said:

"Hey-ho tiddley-pom," in a weary way. "Yes," he replied. "At least, that is what they call me. But they're quite wrong. Actually, I am not abominable at all. In fact, I'm really very civilized. I read a great deal. I have tea at four o'clock every day and I like to sing in the mornings. I also love chocolate. I don't suppose you have any chocolate with you by any chance?"

Now, it just so happened that Paul had a chocolate mouse in his pyjama pocket. He took it out and handed it to the monster. The monster ate it very happily, politely leaving a piece for Paul.

"That was delicious." said the monster kindly. "In return, perhaps you would like me to show you round? There are lots of lovely things to see. But first," he added, disappearing behind the icy peak and re-appearing with a small white fur coat and hat, "you must put this on."

In the white fur outfit, Paul looked just like an Abominable Snowman himself. The monster took Paul's hand. He had a soft furry paw, like a bear, and his nails were beautifully trimmed.

"Do you live here all alone?" asked Paul, as they walked along the snowy mountain path.

"Certainly not!" said the monster in surprise. "That would be very lonely. There are lots of creatures like me, living on all the mountains of the world. Once, a very long time ago, I was a famous mountain climber and lived down below like you. Then I came to the mountain on an expedition and the snow fairies asked me if I would like to stay and help them. The birds, animals and plants up here all need protecting you know, and famous climbers, who know the mountains better than anyone, are ideal for the job. So, by magic, they turned me into the creature I am today." The monster smiled and his moustache turned up.

Then the monster showed Paul some of the creatures he watched over – the arctic fox who runs through the snow valleys of the highest mountains, the snowy owl who flies silently above the tallest peaks, and the magic mountain hare whose fur is as soft as cotton wool and as white as the snow itself. Then he showed Paul how he gave the snowflakes their beautiful patterns, and dusted the ice caps with silver to make them glitter.

"And now it's time for tea!" said the monster, as he led Paul back to his warm cave.

"I once had tea with the famous climber, Sir Edmund Hilary," said the monster as he handed Paul some buttered toast. Suddenly, Paul remembered his great-uncle Edwin. He stared hard at the monster.

"When you were a famous climber, before you became a protector of the mountain, who were you?" he asked.

The monster smiled and picked up a large silver watch from the dresser behind him. He handed it to Paul. On the inside of the lid, engraved in delicate lettering, Paul could just read the name 'Edwin Plank'!

Just at that moment, the watch let out a tiny chime.

"Good heavens!" said the monster. "It's midnight already!" And even while he was still speaking, Paul felt himself starting to grow. The cave began to whirl about him, bathed in the same blinding light as before. And in the distance Paul could faintly hear the voice of the monster calling after him:

"Don't forget the land where the snowy owl flies and the arctic fox runs," it called, again and again, until Paul could hear it no more.

The next moment, Paul found himself back in his bedroom. His present was still wrapped up on the table beside his bed, just as if nothing had happened. Outside, the sun was shining on a snowy landscape. It had been snowing all night long!

Just then, Paul's dad came into the bedroom.

"The snow's too heavy on the mountains," he said smiling. "I got a telegram at the station. So it looks as though I'll be at home for Christmas."

"Hurray!" shouted Paul and ran to hug his dad. As he did so, he realized he was holding something in his hand. There, glittering just like the snow on the tallest ice caps, was great-uncle Edwin's watch. So it hadn't been a dream after all!

When Paul grew up, he became a famous climber, just like his father. And he never forgot the far-off, icy lands where the arctic fox runs and the snowy owl flies. But although he often went looking, he never ever met again that certain, very civilized monster who had tea at four o'clock every day and loved to eat chocolate...

THE END

CECIL THE LAZY DRAGON

by Sally Sheringham

Cecil Dragon was grown up, but he still lived with his parents. Their house was really too small for three large dragons. But it was very neat and tidy — apart from Cecil's room, for Cecil was a very lazy dragon.

"After all," he thought, "why should I bother to rush about tidying my room when I could just stay in bed, reading a comic? Why bother to stand at a stove cooking things to eat, when I could just breathe flames on my food and it would be done in a trice? Why bother to go outdoors when I could just stay in bed all day? In other words, why should I bother to do anything when I could be enjoying doing nothing?"

"What *are* we going to do with you, Cecil Dragon?" his mother would say, sniffing into her handkerchief. "You won't lift a claw to help in the house..."

"Or try to find a job," added his father, his face turning as red as a strawberry. "How can we afford to keep you at home, doing nothing for the rest of your life?"

"And you make the house seem even smaller," sobbed his mother, "always being here."

"You need to be taught a lesson," said his father, sternly. But he couldn't, for the life of him, think what sort of lesson that could be. How could he make Cecil find a job, if he couldn't even get him out of bed?

"Don't worry, parents dear," Cecil would say, airily, shrugging his shoulders. "It'll all work out in the end. And meanwhile, why should I bother to do anything when I can do nothing?"

How unhappy his poor parents were!

One day, as usual, Cecil was lying in bed, reading a comic. His parents were out at work, and he was very happy doing nothing.

"This is the life!" he said, sighing very deeply and very contentedly.

Cecil was too lazy to bother to look around. If he had, he would have noticed that the sparks from his sigh had caused the bedroom curtains to catch fire.

Soon he could smell burning. Then he could hear crackling. He also began to feel much too warm. But Cecil just shrugged. After all, why should he bother to do anything when he could be doing nothing.

But this time Cecil *had* to do something. Flames were leaping up all round him. The whole house had caught fire, including his bed and his comic! If he did nothing a moment longer, he would be burnt to a crisp!

"Snakes alive!" cried Cecil, and just managed to get out of the house before it collapsed in flames.

Cecil was unharmed – apart from his tail, which was smouldering. He went over to the duck pond to cool it down. What a sizzle it made!

When Cecil's parents returned from work they found him still wearing his pyjamas, lying on the front lawn.

This time Cecil had really gone too far. His mother was so upset, she needed twenty handkerchiefs to dry her tears. His father was so angry, his face turned the colour of a raspberry. He shouted at Cecil for a good thirty minutes. But Cecil wasn't even listening!

"Don't worry, dad," he said, when he could get a word in. "It'll all work out in the end."

"How *can* it work out in the end?" roared his father, whose face was now as scarlet as a very, very ripe plum. Something has to be *done* first. And you never *do* anything — except set houses on fire."

"Look," said Cecil. "Why don't you and mum go and stay with Aunt Lucy. Leave everything to me. I have a plan. And now, if you'll excuse me, I have work to do."

"I'll believe that when I see it," muttered his father.

55

But Cecil *did* have a plan. When he had gone to the duck pond to cool down his tail, he had noticed a long line of animals queuing up at Sid Fox's hamburger stall. The animals were getting very cross because Sid Fox was being so slow. Seeing that long queue had given Cecil a very good idea.

Cecil's plan was to set up a hamburger stall of his very own. Above it he put a big sign, "CECIL'S – THE FASTEST FOOD IN TOWN". And it *was* the fastest food in town. All that Cecil had to do was breathe on the food – and it was cooked in a trice! Soon he had made so much money, he could afford to buy his parents a house big enough for at least *ten* full-size dragons!

Cecil's parents were delighted with their new home.

"You've done us proud, son," said his father. And this time his face stayed its normal green colour. His mother even kissed Cecil's cheek.

As for Cecil, he bought himself a double-dragon-sized bed, which he set up beside his stall.

"Why should I bother to do anything, when I can happily do nothing?" he laughed to his customers, as he lay in bed, reading a comic – and cooking ten sausages, four hamburgers and two chicken legs in one hot breath!

THE END

NOEL THE KNOW-ALL GNOME

by Jane Launchbury

Underneath the Christmas tree sat a very odd shaped present. When her husband wasn't looking, Mrs Jones squeezed it, shook it, poked it, and looked at it from all angles, but she couldn't work out what it could possibly be. It was obviously going to be a lovely surprise.

On Christmas morning, Mr Jones picked up the present and gave it to his wife.

"This is for you, darling," he said with a big smile. "I hope you like it."

Mrs Jones took a deep breath and started to tear off the wrapping paper. A bright red shiny hat appeared, with bright yellow spots. Underneath the hat was a bright pink face with a shiny red nose. Mrs Jones gave a gasp as she pulled off the rest of the wrapping paper, for

it revealed the most ghastly garden gnome
she had ever seen! The colours were so
bright that she thought they would
probably glow in the dark.

"I just knew you'd love him,"
said Mr Jones happily. "He's an
Extra-Special-de-Luxe Limited
Edition Gnome," he added,
"of very superior quality.
I thought we could
call him Noel, seeing
that it's Christmas."

"What a good idea," muttered Mrs Jones picking up
the gnome by his big shiny nose and rushing for the back
door. "I can't wait to put him out in the garden."

She hurried down the garden path wondering
wherever her husband could have found quite such a
dreadful creature. She had never liked garden gnomes,
and this one seemed a particularly awful specimen. He
was so unbelievably bright and shiny, and he had a
very snooty smile. Mrs Jones resisted the temptation to
throw the gnome into the pond. She plonked him down
behind a bush instead, and hoped she wouldn't be able
to see him from the house. But Noel's colours were so
bright that he stood out from the rest of the garden like a
sore thumb.

When she had disappeared inside, Noel the gnome stretched his legs and peered down his nose at his new surroundings. He didn't like what he saw. This was no place for a gnome of his superior quality – it was far too dull and dreary. All those boring browns and greens would have to go for a start, and he immediately began planning how he would set about changing things for the better.

If Mrs Jones didn't like the new gnome, the real gnomes and fairies that lived in the garden weren't too pleased either. They had never seen anything quite like Noel before and, as soon as they were sure that there was no one about, they crept out of the trees and bushes to have a closer look. Noel didn't see them coming, of course, because real gnomes and fairies blend in so well with their surroundings that they are almost invisible.

Noel was bending down polishing his shiny shoes until he could see his bright pink face in them, when he realised that there were other faces reflected in them too. He looked up, and for the first time he noticed the gnomes and fairies around him. He sniffed and peered down his nose at the soft grey and brown creatures. They looked to him as though they could all do with a good wash and, being a superior sort of gnome who believed in speaking his mind, he told them so. Then just for good measure, he added that he thought everything in the garden needed a good wash and a few coats of colour, and he was going to have to do something about it. Then he realised that he still hadn't introduced himself.

"My name is Noel, and I'm an Extra-Special-de-Luxe Limited Edition Gnome," he announced grandly.

"Know-all?" said one of the fairies thoughtfully. "That's a very unusual name."

It didn't take long for the fairies and gnomes to decide that "Know-all" was in fact a very good name for the new gnome. He seemed to think he knew everything, and he had a way of looking down his big red nose at everyone that made them feel very uncomfortable. But they were kind creatures so they all decided to try and make him feel at home.

Then one day, Noel pushed his luck a bit too far. He got up very early in the morning, mixed up gallons of brightly coloured paints and set about "improving" the colour scheme in the garden. By the time the other gnomes and fairies realised what he was doing, he had painted all the tree trunks bright orange with turquoise spots, and was cheerfully painting the lawn pink with purple stripes!

The fairies and gnomes were horrified. And they all had to work very hard to put things back to normal before Mr and Mrs Jones woke up! They decided that something had to be done about Noel. But what?

In the end, it was Mrs Jones who dealt with the situation. She had been getting more and more fed up with seeing Noel glowing among the bushes, and on this particular morning he seemed brighter than ever.

"I hate that ugly gnome, he's a real eyesore," she grumbled as she put out some bread for the birds. She knew she couldn't throw him in the dustbin, but she didn't see any harm in temporarily "losing" him. So she looked around the garden for somewhere to hide him, and noticed the compost heap. That would do nicely... She took a big spade and dug a deep hole right in the middle. Then she picked up Noel, dropped him into the hole, and piled the compost back on top of him. The fairies and gnomes couldn't believe their luck.

But the strange thing was that life simply wasn't the same without Noel around. Although he had been an eyesore, and a bossy know-all, most of the fairies and gnomes had to admit that they had admired his enthusiasm and energy. It was just the way he went about things that was all wrong. Even Mrs Jones felt there was something missing from the garden, though she couldn't put her finger on what it was.

At first Noel had been absolutely furious about being buried in the compost heap, but there was nothing he could do about it. Then he started to feel sorry for himself. Deep under the compost, he began to wonder what it was he had done wrong. Perhaps being an Extra-Special-de-Luxe Limited Edition Gnome wasn't quite so wonderful after all. He only knew he was superior because Mr Jones had said so, and what if Mr Jones was wrong? He certainly didn't look like any of the other gnomes. And then there was the matter of the "improvements". Even he had to admit that the garden had looked a bit odd after he tried changing the colour scheme. He was still wondering about this when he heard the sound of digging above him.

Some of the fairies and gnomes had felt so sorry for Noel that they had decided to rescue him. They very nearly missed him, for instead of the bright colours they had been expecting, Noel was coated from head to foot in sticky brown compost.

64

"You look as though you need a good wash!" observed a tall brown gnome. And for once Noel had the sense to say not a word. He was carried over to the pond, where they set about scrubbing the compost off with tiny scrubbing brushes. At first no one noticed what was happening. Then they realised that not only was the compost coming off, but so too were those dreadful bright colours. Underneath, Noel was a lovely

shade of sandy brown. They scrubbed away until all the colours had come off and Noel looked just like an ordinary gnome. He stared at his reflection, and had to admit that it was a distinct improvement. He even heard several fairies comment about his good looks.

No one ever did work out quite what had happened to Noel in the compost heap, but he was a changed character afterwards. Instead of telling everyone what to do, he asked their advice. And when spring came, he learned to love the colours of nature (though he always liked the brighter ones best of all), and he turned out to be a very good gardener.

As for the Joneses, they had the most glorious garden in the village. Mr Jones always said jokingly that it must have been because of Noel, though he had been most upset about the way all his colours had washed off in the rain. Mrs Jones just smiled. She never did work out how he had got out of the compost heap, nor how he had lost his snooty smile and gained a very endearing twinkle in his brown eyes...

THE END

THE WISHING FAIRY

by Andrew Matthews

Sarah and Violet were twins, but they were not at all alike.

Sarah had fair hair and was a kindly girl. While her father and mother were out working on the farm where they lived, Sarah swept the floors and washed the dishes. Violet, on the other hand, had dark hair and was a selfish, vain girl. She was supposed to help with the housework, but instead she stayed in her bedroom, combing her hair and dreaming of the day when a rich and handsome gentleman would carry her off to be his wife. But Sarah was so good-hearted that she never told tales about her lazy sister.

Then one Saturday morning, Mother called Sarah and Violet up to her bedroom. Mother's eyes were watering and her nose was red.

"I've got the most awful cold," she explained. "So I can't take the basket of eggs to market today. You two girls must do it for me."

Now, Violet didn't like this idea at all.

"Ah-choo!" she sneezed. "I think I've caught a cold as well! I must go straight back to bed. Sarah can bring me some warm milk before she leaves for market!" And although Sarah knew her sister was just pretending, she did just that before setting off down the road to town.

It was a hot day. The road was dry and dusty and the basket of eggs made Sarah's arms ache. But instead of complaining to herself, she breathed in the fresh air and listened to the birds singing in the trees and thought what a lovely day it was.

After she had walked for an hour or more, she sat down on some grass at the side of the road to eat the bread and cheese and drink the milk that she had brought with her. She had only just begun her meal, when she noticed someone watching her. It was a little old woman who seemed to have sprung from nowhere. Her clothes were worn, her hair was silver and she leaned on a knobbly black stick.

68

"My!" cried the old lady. "What a hot day it is, and how tired and hungry and thirsty I am!"

Sarah instantly felt sorry for the old woman.

"Sit next to me grandmother," she said politely. "You can rest on the soft grass and share my food and drink if you like."

"What a kind girl you are!" exclaimed the old woman, and she sat down as Sarah had suggested. When she had finished eating and drinking, the old woman winked at Sarah.

"What would you say if I told you that I was a fairy?" she asked. Sarah thought for a moment.

"I would believe you grandmother, for you have such a kind face," she replied.

"Prettily answered!" chuckled the old lady. "And you would be right to do so, for I am the Wishing Fairy! Now, take my stick and tap it on the ground three times, then see what happens."

Sarah did as she was told and tapped the stick on the ground. One! Two! Three! All at once, the eggs flew out of the basket and broke in half on the ground. But instead of the usual yellow yolk, out poured all sorts of wonderful things. Ruby rings, silver combs, silk scarves and a leather purse full of gold coins lay on the road.

"These things are all yours," said the Wishing Fairy. "They are a reward for your kindness and I hope they bring you happiness."

Overjoyed, Sarah gathered up the treasures and ran home.

Her mother and father were amazed when they heard all about Sarah's adventure. Violet was terribly jealous.

"Little Miss Goody-Goody!" she muttered to herself. "I bet I can do better than her." And, forgetting she was supposed to have a cold, she put some eggs in a basket, along with some good things to eat and drink, and set off down the road to town.

It was still a hot day, and before long Violet longed to sit down.

"I will not stop until I see the old woman," she said to herself, and forced herself to walk on. But she hadn't gone much farther before she was saying, "Bother the silly old nuisance! Why doesn't she appear? I'm sure Sarah didn't have to walk this far!" And not long after that she said, "I can't go on. This is really too unfair. I must sit down and have something to eat and drink!"

So she sat down at the side of the road and unpacked the hamper of food she had brought with her. Out came ham and cold chicken, fresh bread, cream cakes and some cool milk to drink.

Before she had time to eat anything, Violet noticed a young girl watching her from the other side of the road. She was dressed in rags and was leaning on a knobbly old stick.

"What do you want?" said Violet rudely, carefully unwrapping some juicy tomatoes.

"My!" cried the child. "What a hot day it is and how tired and hungry and thirsty I am!"

"Serves you right!" said Violet, stuffing a piece of chicken into her mouth. "You should have packed something to bring with you as I did."

"I see," said the girl. "And what would you say if I told you that I was the Wishing Fairy that your sister met this morning?"

Now, Violet was quite taken aback by this, but she soon recovered her senses.

"My sister told me all about you," she said. "So give me that stick at once! I want some silk scarves too, and emerald rings instead of ruby ones, and gold combs instead of silver!"

72

So saying, she grabbed the stick and banged it three times upon the ground. The eggs in her basket flew into the air. But instead of breaking on the ground to reveal the beautiful treasures Violet expected, they smashed over her head, covering her from head to foot in slimy, smelly egg yolk. When she looked up, there before her stood the old woman, leaning on her stick and chuckling merrily.

"I want my reward!" wailed Violet.

"You've got just what you deserved, my girl!" laughed the old woman. "Let this be a lesson to you." And with that, the stick flew up into the air and began to whack Violet hard. She ran home as fast as she could, with the stick chasing her all the way. But when she got to the front gate, it vanished into thin air with a whoosh.

After that, Violet mended her ways. She helped Sarah with the housework and stopped being so lazy and horrid. In the end, her dream came true – she did marry a rich, handsome gentleman. And so did Sarah. But those are two different stories...

THE END

FLORENCE AND WILFRED

by Sally Sheringham

Florence was an elderly fairy. She lived in a snug little cottage with her best friend, a marmalade cat called Wilfred. Florence was very happy on the whole, except every now and then she longed to be young and beautiful again.

"But I like you just the way you are," Wilfred would say, and Florence would reply that a cat — and a *male* cat, at that — couldn't possibly understand how she felt.

For Florence's 195th birthday, Wilfred gave her a pair of warm, sensible slippers.

"It's very kind of you, Wilfred dear," sighed Florence, "but these slippers make me feel even older." Then Florence suddenly had a brilliant idea. "I know!" she exclaimed. "I'll give myself a birthday present — I'll use my magic to become young and beautiful again.

Don't you think that's a brilliant idea Wilfred?"

"Humph," said Wilfred. "I think it's a very unbrilliant idea if you ask me." And he stalked off with his nose in the air.

The 'Young and Beautiful' spell turned out to be very complicated and Florence missed having Wilfred to help her. She had to find unpleasant ingredients like slugs, bugs and other slimy things too nasty to mention.

At last everything was assembled in a saucepan. She waved her magic wand. There was a bright blue flash and the concoction started to boil and smoke.

When it cooled down she poured the potion into a silver goblet and drank it. It tasted as revolting as it looked.

"I suppose even fairies have to suffer to be beautiful," Florence sighed, pulling a face.

Then she went upstairs, stood in front of the mirror and waited. She felt rather nervous...

75

Suddenly the magic started! FIZZ! Her straight white hair turned jet black and started to curl. WHIZZ! Her wrinkled cheeks and crumpled wings turned as smooth as if they'd just been ironed. ZIZZ! Her plump, cuddly body turned sleek and curvy.

Wilfred, who had heard all the fizzing and whizzing from the garden, watched disapprovingly from the doorway.

"Just look at me," Florence gasped. "I must be the most beautiful fairy in the world. Er – you don't think I've overdone the spell a bit, do you Wilfred?"

"A *bit*?" growled Wilfred. "That's putting it mildly. It's bound to lead to trouble if you ask me." But Florence just ignored him.

"I feel pretty – oh so pretty," she sang, twirling round and round in a cornflower blue dress she hadn't been able to fit into since she was eighteen.

"Humph," said Wilfred. "Personally, I preferred you the way you were." But Florence just told him not to be such a spoilsport.

During her birthday tea, Florence kept rushing off to the mirror to admire herself. She hardly ate any of the pink cake Wilfred had baked for her.

"It's delicious, Wilfred dear, but I don't want to spoil my new slim figure," she said, tossing her black curls.

"Humph," said Wilfred again.

But there was one thing Florence had overlooked in her desire to be young and beautiful – and that was that all the goblins and elves and gnomes for miles around would fall in love with her. It wasn't long before they were queuing at her door! In just one week she received ten boxes of chocolates, nine bunches of flowers, eight gold rings and seven offers of marriage.

Soon Florence spent all her time being wooed by doting admirers and having sweet nothings whispered in her ear.

"I might as well be a bit of furniture for the amount of interest she's showing in me," Wilfred thought sulkily as he sat alone by the fire.

The weeks went by and after a while Florence grew tired of being chased by all the gnomes, goblins and elves. She couldn't even go shopping without would-be husbands pursuing her, and the sweet nothings were getting extremely boring. Then one night she had a horrible dream about being married to a particularly ugly elf and, when she woke up, it suddenly struck her that Wilfred was better company than all her admirers put together.

The next morning Florence and Wilfred were enjoying a quiet breakfast together when, all of a sudden, a fat gnome started to recite love poems through the window. If that wasn't bad enough, a bald goblin with a box of chocolates started to bang on the door, and a lanky elf tried to climb down the chimney with a bunch of red roses.

"Oh, Wilfred, we can't even have breakfast in peace any more," cried Florence sadly. "My nerves won't stand it. Please send them away before I go mad."

Wilfred rose to his full height. The marmalade hairs on his back stood on end and his whiskers bristled.

"My mistress won't be receiving visitors today, or tomorrow, or ever again," Wilfred announced in his most important voice. "So may I bid you gentlemen good-day?"

Wilfred could look quite fierce when he wanted to; he certainly did then, and Florence's suitors hurried off. "I have to admit that being young and beautiful has a few disadvantages," said Florence with a sigh. "Would you mind helping me change back into my old self, Wilfred dear?"

79

"It would be a pleasure," said Wilfred.

Together they prepared the magic potion. This time, it tasted even more revolting! Then – FIZZ! Florence's curly black hair turned straight and white. WHIZZ! Her wrinkles returned. ZIZZ! Her body became lumpy and cuddly again.

Her suitors were all very puzzled. Whatever had happened to the young, beautiful fairy?

"She's gone away – for good," Wilfred told them firmly.

That evening, Florence and Wilfred sat cosily by the fire playing Snap. Florence wore her birthday slippers and munched a cream doughnut because she no longer had to worry about her figure. Wilfred was purring.

"I've just decided, Wilfred dear, that I really rather like being old and ugly," said Florence. "It's so much more restful."

"And the company's better," said Wilfred dryly. "Snap!"

THE END

THE
ELF BULL

by Andrew Matthews

Farmer Hardacre charged into the kitchen panting and puffing and all of a dither.

"You'll never guess what I've found, Meg!" he told his astonished wife. "No, not if you guess for the next hundred years!"

"I shan't waste my time trying then!" snapped Mrs Hardacre. "You'd best tell me and have done with it." Without more ado, Farmer Hardacre slipped his knapsack off his shoulder, placed it on the kitchen table and opened it.

Inside the knapsack was a tiny bull, no bigger than a kitten. Its coat was black and glossy, its horns and hooves shone like silver, and its eyes glowed as red as two splinters of ruby. A fine gold chain was fastened around its neck like a collar.

"I found it caught in the thorn hedge down the lane," explained Farmer Hardacre. "I couldn't believe my eyes.

Did you ever see the like in all your born days?"

Mrs Hardacre went quite pale.

"Jack!" she whispered. "You take that creature back where you found it this very minute."

"But, Meg..."

"No buts, Jack!" insisted Mrs Hardacre. "That be an Elf Bull and Elf Bulls belong to the Elves!"

"'Tis mine," said the farmer stubbornly. "I found it! And I mean to take this fine little chap to market right away. I reckon some fancy lord or lady would pay a pretty penny for a poppet like this! Put on your finest dress, Meg, for we're off to town."

"Not me!" said Mrs Hardacre, shaking her head. "I'll have no part of such foolishness! Elves be tricky little things. No good will come of it, Jack, you mark my words!" But Farmer Hardacre chose to ignore his wife's warning. He bustled off to the stable, hitched up the pony and trap and set off on the road to town.

82

Before long, he met a strange little man perching on a milestone at the side of the road. His boots, breeches and jerkin were bright green, his face was nut-brown and his eyes twinkled merrily. But the strangest thing about him was his ears – for they were long and pointed.

"Oh-ho!" thought Farmer Hardacre as he reined his pony to a halt, for he knew an Elf when he saw one.

"Good day, Farmer Hardacre!" said the little man.

"Good day, Master Elf! And what can I do for you?" replied Farmer Hardacre in his most polite voice.

"You've got something that belongs to me in that old knapsack of yours," said the Elf.

"What's mine is mine!" returned the farmer rudely. "Finders keepers!"

But instead of getting cross, the Elf smiled.

"If you be a friend to the Elves, they'll be friends to you," he said. "But if you steal what belongs to them, woe betide you!"

"Hah!" scoffed the farmer even more rudely. "I'm off to market to do business, and talking to you is just a waste of time! Do your worst, little green fellow!" So saying, the farmer grasped the reins of his pony and continued on his way.

"It won't be as easy as you think...," he heard the Elf call after him, but he shrugged off the words and set his mind back to thinking of a purse fat with gold coins. After all, what could the Elves possibly do to a big strong farmer like him.

Town was busy and it took Farmer Hardacre a long time to find the spot he wanted. It was right in the middle of the town square, next to the horse-trough. He hitched up his pony, then stood up in the trap and started shouting to attract attention.

"Roll up, roll up! Come and take the chance of a lifetime!" he cried. "Have your money ready! Feast your eyes on an amazing sight!"

Farmer Hardacre bawled so loudly that before long a large crowd had gathered around him.

"What I've got for sale is one of the wonders of the world!" announced the farmer. "You'll see something that'll make your eyes pop out. In years to come you'll tell your grandchildren about what I'm carrying in my knapsack!"

"Show us then!" called someone in the crowd. Farmer Hardacre held up his hand for silence.

"You must prepare yourselves," he warned, "for no-one here will have seen the like before, no, nor ever will again, I daresay!"

So saying, he placed his hand in the knapsack, closed his fingers around what he felt inside and drew it out for all to see.

"There now!" he cried. "Seeing is believing!" But to his dismay, instead of the astonished gasps he had expected, the crowd burst into peals of laughter. The farmer glanced at his hand and saw, not the Elf Bull, but a string of pork sausages. So the Elves had got their own back after all.

"Swindled by magic!" he cursed. Farmer Hardacre became so angry, that the crowd, laughing, threw him in the horse-trough to cool him down.

The farmer drove home a sadder, wiser and wetter man. When he reached the milestone, he found the Elf still waiting.

"I told you it wouldn't be easy, Farmer Hardacre!"

"Huh!" grunted the farmer.

"Cheer up!" smiled the Elf. "It could have been worse. Why, the Elf Bull might have turned into a tiger and eaten you up!"

"I suppose so!" mumbled the farmer. "Well, I'm very sorry and I wish I could give you your bull back. But all I have left is a string of sausages." The Elf laughed and his eyes twinkled.

"Just look in the bag again," he chuckled. And when Farmer Hardacre opened it up, why, there was the Elf Bull with its shiny black coat and glittering red eyes.

"Well, I'll be blowed!" said the farmer with a smile. And gently he put the bag down on the ground.

The Bull was delighted to be back with the Elf. It frisked and snorted and tapped its silver hooves on the road. Farmer Hardacre gathered up the pony's reins and started to head for home.

"Farewell, Elf-Friend!" cried the Elf after him. "I'm glad to see you've learnt your lesson."

"And much good may it do me," sighed the farmer.

And much good it *did* do him, for in the years that followed the farmer's fields produced the finest grain, and his cows produced the thickest cream for miles around.

"One good turn deserves another!" chuckled Farmer Hardacre to himself.

And it's certain that if he ever found any Elf Bulls after that, he left them well alone.

THE END

THE GOBLINS OF GRIDDLESTONE GAP

by Philip Steele

Bob Goblin and Slob Goblin were hobgoblins, and they knew everything that went on at Griddlestone Gap. Why, there had been hobgoblins in the Gap since giants lived in the forest and wolves ran free on the hills. Now, for those of you who don't know, hobgoblins are always up to one mischief or another. And at Griddlestone Gap it was no different. Their long, bony fingers lifted latches and knocked on doors, or scrabbled at windows to frighten honest people. Children would pull bedclothes over their heads and say:

> "Gribbledy, grobbledy goblins,
> Mean as mean can be!
> Gribbledy, grobbledy goblins,
> Don't say boo to me!"

88

This was a bit unfair, because goblins were not really *mean*, just very, very naughty.

Bob Goblin and Slob Goblin were twins, and young twins at that, for they were only 303½ years old. And over the years they had got up to all kinds of tricks. They had tied together the parson's shoelaces, so that he tripped over as he climbed into the pulpit. They had moved a scarecrow from the field and set it down by the fire in the local inn. And they had removed all the pegs so the tents collapsed at the village fête. How the villagers had gawped!

Of the two, Slob Goblin was the craftiest, and clever with it: he could write rhymes in perfect Gobbledegook and cast spells on special days of the year. Bob Goblin was the most handsome: he had the bandiest legs, the most pointed ears, and eyes which glowed like Hallowe'en lanterns.

One fine morning, Bob and Slob were sitting on a gate, sucking some eggs they had sneaked from the henhouse.

"Have you heard, Slob?" said Bob.

"Heard what, Bob?" said Slob.

"They've built a new house at the end of Griddlestone Gap."

"Oh they have, have they?" said Slob, arching his eyebrows. He began to giggle and then to cackle. "Shall we goblinize them, then?" he croaked gleefully. And with that the hobgoblins went into a huddle and whispered secretly to each other.

89

That evening, Mr Mulberry was taking the air outside his splendid new house. The thatch was trim, the timbers strong and the garden as neat and tidy as could be. "Mr Mulberry of Griddlestone Hall," he said to himself, savouring the sound of the words with pride. Then suddenly, out of the corner of his eye, he thought he saw something slip through the grass, and a window rattled behind him.

"Mrs M!" he bellowed, striding back indoors. "Did you hear something just then?"

"Not a thing, dearest!" said his wife as she came out of the dining hall. "Now come and eat your supper, or it will get cold."

Inside, the table was piled high with Mr Mulberry's favourite dishes. He eased himself into a chair, and leaned forward to sniff the yellow roses which decorated the table.

"Wa–aa–aa–haa–haa–SHOO!!!" Mr Mulberry sneezed. "Pepper!" he exclaimed when he'd recovered enough to talk. "There's pepper on those roses or I'm a cabbage!"

"Don't be ridiculous, dearest," said Mrs Mulberry with a pitying look. "You've probably got a cold coming. Now then, have a nice bowl of soup."

As she lifted the lid of the tureen, a green frog leaped out, hopped across the tablecloth and out of the window. Mr Mulberry screamed.

Their first meal at Griddlestone Hall was not a success. There was ink in the gravy boat, salt in the custard, and cod liver oil in the port. And that was not all. When he went to bed, Mr Mulberry found spiders in his nightcap, and the bedclothes turned over at both ends. All night long there was a squeaking and a creaking, a hammering and a yammering. By four in the morning, he could stand it no more.

"Hobgoblins!" he shouted. Mrs M awoke with a start.

"I *beg* your pardon?" she said.

"Hobgoblins!" repeated Mr Mulberry. "If this isn't the work of hobgoblins, my name is not Marmaduke Mulberry! And *I* am going to catch them!"

Mr Mulberry put on his slippers and he put on his
dressing gown, and he crept downstairs. In the pantry he
could see a candle burning. He tiptoed in very softly.
There were Bob Goblin and Slob Goblin, bold as brass,
sitting on a barrel of apricots.

In a trice, Mr Mulberry tipped them in and slammed the
lid down on the barrel. Carrying it over his shoulder, he
ran out into the garden and threw it down the well.

"And that is the end of *that*!" he said triumphantly.

But Mr Mulberry knew little of hobgoblin habits. To
a goblin, a well is the most perfect little home
imaginable.

"Just the place to settle down," said Bob Goblin to
Slob Goblin, climbing from the barrel and sitting on a
stone ledge.

"Home, sweet home!" said Slob Goblin to Bob
Goblin, as he spat out an apricot stone.

93

So for many a long year the happy hobgoblins lived in the well at Griddlestone Hall, and they were so busy tidying up their new home that they hardly had time to play pranks. They still live there today, it is said, but now they are old and grey, and sleep away the days. But once in a while, visitors to the hall hear knocks and bangs in the wainscotting, and window panes rattle on windless nights. And the children in the village still pull bedclothes over their heads and say:

"Gribbledy, grobbledy goblins,
Mean as mean can be!
Gribbledy, grobbledy goblins,
Don't say boo to me!"

THE END

THE WORLD'S GREATEST LEPRECHAUN HUNT

by Deborah Tyler

F ar away, in a land which was known as the Emerald Isle, there was a kingdom. It was a small kingdom and it was very poor. Its farms never seemed to thrive and even its castle was shabby. The only person in the kingdom who seemed to thrive was Prince James. He was the son of King Merrow and Queen Mag, and he was very spoiled. When he did not get just what he wanted, he would let out a high pitched squeal and start throwing things. As the Court Jester had once pointed out, he was really quite nasty.

Now the kingdom of King Merrow and Queen Mag was surrounded by magic woods. Sometimes, when people passed through them, they could hear strange laughter. And often visitors felt as if they were being followed by many pairs of tiny eyes or heard the patter of tiny footsteps among the leaves. If they had been quick enough and nimble on their feet, they might have caught a glimpse of a green velvet waistcoat or the flash of a bushy red beard. For the magic wood was the home of the Leprechauns who had lived on the Emerald Isle for years and years and years.

For those of you who have never seen a Leprechaun before, they are very small and wear three-cornered hats, smart breeches, red shirts and green velvet waistcoats with shiny buttons. But the most striking thing about them is their hair, for it is always long and red and matches their bushy beards perfectly.

Now Leprechauns are tricky little creatures and usually keep well out of the way of humans, which isn't always easy. For there is a legend in the Emerald Isle that if you catch a Leprechaun and look him in the eye, a crock of gold and three wishes could be yours.

At the time of our story, Prince James had come of age, but this did not stop him from throwing the most terrible tantrums! If the King asked him to do something, he usually shouted "Shan't" and pulled a face. He was sulking terribly on the day of his birthday because he wanted to have a huge birthday party and his mother and father couldn't afford it. They had spoiled him for so long, they had no money left.

"It's no good," the King said one day. "We need a crock of gold. We shall have to capture a Leprechaun! Send for my knights." So, the best knights in the kingdom were sent for and they all set out on what came to be known as "The World's Greatest Leprechaun Hunt".

Leprechauns are mischievous little men and they love practical jokes better than anything. So as soon as they heard that the knights were coming to track them down, they prepared many traps. The most tricky Leprechaun in the forest was called King Sean and he had a beautiful daughter called Mora, who was as lovely and as tiny as a china doll. Mora had often seen the knights before as they rode through the woods with the Prince. She was secretly in love with Prince James and owned a large picture of him.

"The World's Greatest Leprechaun Hunt" was not exactly a great triumph. One knight had followed a little man into a glade. He had stood behind a tree, preparing to pounce while the Leprechaun lit a clay pipe. Then, when he actually tried to grab his victim, he found that another little man had fastened him to the tree with strong twine.

Another knight had been chased home by four little men who had pelted him with hundreds of tiny shoes. As Leprechauns make shoes, they had a great supply. Other knights had vanished down holes, landing in thick mud when they got to the bottom. Twine and leaves had been made into catapults, which shot berries at them, and Leprechauns swung down on vines with cakes of mud that made a nasty mess of their armour. In fact, when the Prince walked over to see how the "Great Hunt" was progressing, he was almost trampled on by knights who were running away.

"Come back," shouted the Prince, but the knights just kept on running. Prince James leant against a tree. "It's all my fault that the kingdom is poor," he said to himself. "But what on earth can I do to put things right?" Just then he heard a tiny voice.

"Please sir," it said, "I can help you." James looked up and saw Mora standing before him. She was the smallest and prettiest girl that he had ever seen. "I can find you a Leprechaun," she said. "My father is their King." So saying, she took the Prince by the hand and led him to her father. When her father heard her step, he turned round and looked James straight in the eye. Thus it was that Prince James could claim a crock of gold and three wishes.

"Well!" said Sean crossly. "Name your first wish."

The Prince thought hard and, though he knew he should do otherwise, he decided that the kingdom could wait.

"I want a new horse," he said. There was a flash of emerald light and a lovely white horse stood before him. "I wanted a black one," said James rudely. The Leprechaun went red in the face.

"What is your second wish?" he said angrily.

"A new coat," said James, who had decided that the kingdom could wait until last. There was a flash of blue light and a brilliant sapphire coat appeared upon the Prince's back, which fastened itself up rather neatly.

"It's too tight," whined the Prince.

"NO!" said the Leprechaun King, bristling with rage. "You are too FAT! I am tired of your moanin' and groanin' and will not grant your last wish until you take me to the palace." Then he jumped upon the horse and got Mora

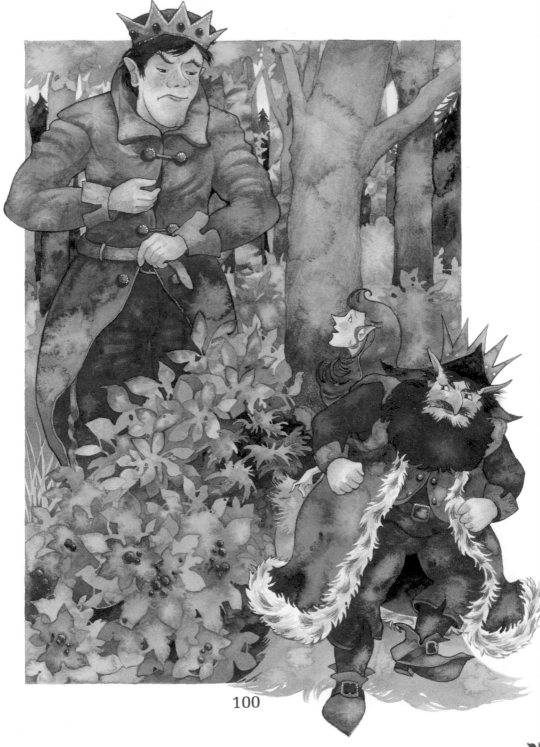

and James to do the same.

They rode to the court and when they got there, King Sean told Mag and Merrow the whole story. The King and Queen were ashamed of their son's behaviour and were sorry that he was so spoiled. In short, they wished to teach him a lesson, but they didn't know how.

"I will give you one last wish and the crock of gold if I can have a wish of my own granted," said the little man. The King and Queen agreed and their son sulked.

So, under much protest, the Prince asked for a prosperous kingdom. When he had done so, all the castle shook and there was a blinding ray of pink light before their eyes. When it had gone, the castle gleamed as if it had been painted, the grass glowed a rich, emerald green, and the flowers in all the window boxes blossomed like jewels. On all the farms, the cattle grew fat and crops grew tall.

"Now for my wish," said the little man. "I want your son to marry my daughter, as she loves him – although I wish I knew why." The royal couple agreed at once for they thought Mora was lovely, and the Prince, well, he just sulked.

The wedding date was set without the consent of the Prince. The castle chapel was decorated with glittering paper shamrocks, pale green candles, and berries and wild roses from the forest. On the day of the wedding, Mora wore a lovely gown of woven water lilies and spiders' webs. The Prince was so cross about the whole affair that he had gone purple in the face, which really matched his robes very well. The ceremony was about to begin, and knights and Leprechauns filled the pews, when Mora cried,

"Stop!" The whole court was silent. "I cannot marry you, unless you love me for myself," she continued. "Your selfishness has made everyone unhappy, even you. Now it is time you started behaving like a proper prince." Suddenly James realised how dreadful he had been. He thought of his poor father and mother and how awful

he had been to everyone. Above all, he saw how horrid he had been to Mora, who had loved him so unselfishly, when really he had secretly loved her all along!

"I will marry you Mora," said James, "and I will be a well-loved prince!" Mora smiled and so the wedding ceremony began. And when James finally kissed his bride, she grew to be as tall as he was. King Sean went back to his home in the magic woods, though he always went to the castle for tea on Sundays, and the Leprechauns carried on playing tricks on anyone who went looking for crocks of gold behind the trees. Even today, if you should ever travel to the Emerald Isle and walk through the woods there, you just might be lucky enough to hear Leprechaun laughter from among the trees or catch a climpse of a bushy red beard, or a velvet waistcoat fastened with shiny buttons.

THE END

EDWARD AND ANNA

by Jane Launchbury

F ar away, at the edge of a great mountain range, there lived a poor woman and her two children, a boy called Edward, and a girl called Anna. Two winters ago, their loving father had set off to hunt deer in the mountains, but there had been a terrible avalanche and he had never returned. Every night the children lit a lamp in the tiny cottage window, in the hope that it would guide him home; but all that ever came were big furry moths, spinning dizzily towards the light.

One dark night there was a terrible storm in the mountains. Lightning flashed across the sky, thunder crashed, and echoes rumbled down the valleys. Edward and Anna rushed into their mother's room and huddled against her in bed. Outside, the rain lashed against the

windows, and the wild wind howled angrily through the trees and down the chimney. The lamp at the cottage window flared and flickered, sending eerie shadows dancing over the walls, but it didn't go out.

"Don't worry," said the children's mother, cuddling them to her, "it's only a horrid old storm. It'll soon go away."

But the storm got worse and worse. Suddenly, a great thunder crash was followed by a terrible creaking and screaming, as though a vast monster was heading straight for them. The old chestnut tree behind the cottage was tearing its roots from the ground. It seemed to fall in slow motion on to the little cottage. There was a horrible sound as roof timbers smashed. Tiles flew in all direction. Twigs, tiles and rain poured in through a gaping hole. The children and their mother took refuge in the old woodshed. At least it was dry in there. All night the storm raged, but at the cottage window the lamp burned steadily on.

When daylight came, and the last rumbles of thunder had vanished over the mountains, the family crept out of the woodshed. They looked gloomily at their home. There was very little left of the roof. Sadly, they walked around the soggy rooms, looking up at the brightening sky through the gaping hole.

"Whatever are we going to do?" sighed Anna. She knew that they could not afford a new roof. Then she had an idea. Once she had gone up into the mountains with her father to gather reeds from beside a great blue lake. "I know," she gasped. "We can cut reeds and thatch the roof ourselves."

So, as soon as the sun had fully risen, the children's mother gave them a bag with the last small scraps of bread and cheese. She told them to keep to the paths and hurry back home before dark. Then she waved goodbye and Edward and Anna set off for the lake in the mountains.

For hours the children walked up winding paths that lead higher and higher into the mountains. At last they saw the great blue lake, shimmering in a valley below them and they ran cheerfully towards it.

Around the edges of the lake grew the tall reeds that Anna had remembered. The reeds grew most thickly in a dark inlet, shadowed by a mountain crag. Edward and Anna settled down to work there straight away. It was much quicker than cutting the reeds that grew in the sunshine, but there was a chilly feel to the place. Soon they became aware of another sound above the croaking of the mountain frogs which were all around them. It sounded like a wheezy voice whispering something. Edward and Anna stopped work and looked around.

They couldn't see anyone. Then they heard the voice again. This time it was much clearer.

> *"Swish, swosh, who DARES to take,*
> *Reeds that grow in MY lake?"*

A bony old woman crept out of the shadows. She was the ugliest person they had ever seen. She was bent over a stick and, as she hobbled closer, the children saw that her skin was a sort of greenish yellow.

Anna and Edward backed away, but there was no escape. Behind them, there was only the tangled reed bed and the deep blue lake. Around them, the mountain frogs had begun to croak in unison. They seemed to be saying something: "Beware of the Witch of the Lake," they croaked over and over again.

Then the old woman spoke, in quite a friendly voice.

"You must be hungry my little chickens. Come into my house and I'll give you a nice meal. Then you'll be strong enough to cut as many reeds as you need."

Edward and Anna were a little comforted by this, but still they didn't move.

"Come along my little froglets," she said, edging towards them.

This time they didn't have any choice. Taking them by the hands, the old woman led the two children into her house. Outside, the frogs croaked louder than ever.

"Here, child. Help me light the fire," she crooned to Anna. "Then I can cook you a real feast. You, boy. Go and fetch fresh water from the well outside and fill this pot," she said, pointing a crooked finger at a vast cauldron. "Hurry now."

Edward went gloomily out to the well. He did not trust the old woman, but he couldn't just run off and leave his sister. He leaned over the well and sighed heavily. It was a very deep well, and his sigh echoed around and around its depths. Then he heard another sound.

On a ledge just inside the well shaft, there sat a handsome green frog with shiny yellow eyes. Drops of water glittered on its back, like jewels. It looked up at Edward and spoke:

"The old woman is a wicked witch. She is going to eat you up. You must trick her and escape."

"Oh no!" gasped Edward. "How can I trick her?" Then he had an idea. "How deep is the well?" he asked.

"Deeper than the night," replied the frog, pushing a little pebble down the shaft. Edward waited to hear the

109

splash as it hit the water. When it eventually came, the sound was so faint that he could only just hear it.

"Stay there kind frog. Keep croaking as loudly as you can," he said. Then he ran back to the witch's house.

"Come outside," called Edward. "There's a huge fat frog in the well. It would make a delicious meal." The old witch needed no further bidding, and she lurched over to the well. Anna ran after her. The little frog was hiding in a crack, and croaking with all its might.

The old witch peered into the depths of the well, but she couldn't see any huge, fat frogs.

"It's down there," said Edward, pointing into the darkness. "Can't you see it?" The old woman leaned even further into the well, licking her lips.

"Now!" shouted Edward. "Push!" He and Anna gave the witch a great shove.

The witch let out a shriek and toppled over into the well. Down, down, she tumbled. Edward listened for the splash. At last it came. The echoes lasted for quite a while, then all was quiet. The wicked witch had gone forever. Then, out of the gloom, they heard the croaking of the frog. Edward leaned into the well, and lifted the little creature out in his hands.

"Thank you, frog," he whispered. Then he kissed it gently on the top of its head.

There was a blinding flash, and the little frog turned into a tall man.

"Anna! Edward!" he cried.

"Father!" gasped the children, rushing into his arms. "We thought you had been swept away forever in the avalanche," said Anna.

"No," said their father. "The wicked witch caught

me. She turned me into a frog for her supper, but I escaped and I've been living here in the well ever since. You must have broken the spell." Then the children told their father about the great storm, that had destroyed their roof, and how they had come to gather reeds by the lake. "Oh my clever, brave children!" cried their father. "We must collect the reeds and get home to your mother as fast as we can."

It was nearly dark as they set off down the stony paths. As the sky got darker, a tiny glow from the foot of the mountain got stonger. The children's mother had lit the lamp in the cottage window, and its light drew them all back to home and safety at last.

THE END

THE MAGIC ISLAND

by Elizabeth Waugh

F ar, far away, in the warm South Seas, there is a magic island, ruled over by a kindly witch called Thomasina Toffee. On Thomasina's island the sea shells are made of bubblegum, the streams flow with sparkling lemonade and huge chocolate buttons grow on the trees. For Thomasina had a sweet tooth, and there was nothing she liked better than to nibble a tasty little sweet. As she was a witch, and her teeth were made of good strong crystal, she never needed any fillings, and could eat as many sweets as she liked. Thomasina's broomstick was made of barley sugar, and every day she would ride on it around her island, flying high over the cream soda waterfalls and the toffee trees.

One night, when Thomasina was fast asleep in her marzipan bed, she was woken suddenly by the sound of

112

the wind howling and the waves crashing on the shore. There was a terrible storm. The wind was blowing so hard that the chocolate buttons were pitter-pattering down from the trees, and the pear drop sea shells were being whirled along the beach.

Crossly, Thomasina got out of bed, put on her magic spangled cloak and made her way down to the beach. She tried to make a spell to calm the storm, but her magic was not strong enough. In the distance she could see a ship rolling and heaving on the waves. She was a good witch and would liked to have helped, but there was nothing she could do. So she went back to her little toffee house, shut the door firmly, and got into bed.

When she woke in the morning, the sun was shining and the sea was calm and still. She was drinking her breakfast cup of hot chocolate when suddenly she heard a loud:

"ACHOOO!"

It came from the beach. But who could it be? Nobody else lived on Thomasina's island. She quickly jumped on her barley sugar broomstick and flew down to the sea-shore. There, sitting on a rock and looking very cold, wet and bedraggled, was a little yellow teddy bear.

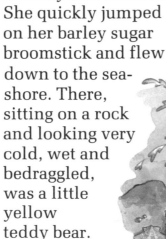

"Achooo!" he sneezed and spluttered and shivered. Thomasina floated down beside him.

"Zimblebee-fiddle-me-dee!" she said. "And who are you?"

"My name is – ACHOOO! – Ernest Pumpkin," said the little teddy bear. "I was sailing with my family on a big ship, and I got washed overboard in a terrible storm."

"Well, my dear Mr Pumpkin," said Thomasina, kindly. "Welcome to my magic island! You must come back to my house to dry yourself!"

"Please call me Ernest," said the teddy bear. "Thank you for your kind invitation. I should very much like to dry myself. ACHOOO!"

So Ernest climbed on the back of Thomasina's broomstick, and back they flew to her little toffee house.

The sun was shining, and Ernest soon dried off. Thomasina offered him all sorts of delicious things to eat: a thimble-full of raspberryade, a slice of fudge, a little plate of chocolate buttons. Then she took him on a lovely ride around the island, and showed him the cream soda waterfall and the pear drop sea shells. That evening Thomasina gave him his own little bed and Ernest slept better than ever before.

Ernest loved sweets too, so he had a wonderful time on Thomasina's magic island. He stayed for several weeks, steadily growing fatter and fatter. But one day Thomasina noticed that he was looking very sad. He hadn't bothered to eat his breakfast, and he was sitting gloomily on the doughnut sofa staring ahead of him. Then a fat tear rolled down his cheek and plopped onto the floor.

"Whatever is the matter, Ernest?" asked Thomasina, anxiously.

"I miss my family," said Ernest, sadly, "and especially Jennifer, the little girl who owned me. I wonder where she is now? She must miss me too!"

"Well, let's have a look in my crystal ball," said Thomasina. "Then we can see what they are all doing."

Thomasina brought a beautiful, shining, round object out of her cupboard. "It's magic," she explained. "If you look into it, you can see where your friends are and what they are doing."

Thomasina placed it carefully on the table and said her magic spell:

> *"Crystal ball, shining bright,*
> *Through the day and through the night,*
> *Tell me where is Jennifer now?"*

As they peered into the crystal ball, shapes slowly began to form. "Why, look!" cried Ernest. "It's Jennifer! And her mother! They're in a house by the seaside!"

"Well, that's easy!" said Thomasina. "I can take you there on my broomstick. But we will have to go at night, so that nobody sees us. And we had better wear my spangled cloak, in case it gets cold."

So, that very night, Thomasina and Ernest set off on the barley sugar broomstick. They whizzed through the moonlight, over islands and oceans, until they came to the house where Ernest's family was staying. They floated down on the broomstick and landed in the garden. As quietly as a little mouse, Thomasina opened the back door by magic, and Ernest tiptoed into the sitting room and jumped onto the sofa. He kissed Thomasina goodbye, and thanked her very much for her kindness. Then she climbed back onto the broomstick and flew back home to her magic island.

When Jennifer came down for breakfast the following morning, she was amazed to see Ernest sitting on the sofa. She rushed up to him, and hugged and kissed him.

"Mummy! Mummy!" she yelled. "Guess what! Ernest has come back! Come and see!"

And so Ernest returned to live happily with his family. But as he sat in the nursery with the other toys, eagerly waiting for Jennifer to bring some crumpets for tea, he often thought of the kindly witch Thomasina and her magic island, where all those good things to eat could be had if you just stretched out your paw.

And, as for Jennifer, she never understood why Ernest had grown so fat...

THE END

WITCH WURZEL

by Elizabeth Waugh

Witch Wurzel lived in a dark, smelly cave on Bald Mountain. Her cat, Snout, helped her with her spells, but he was simply not good enough. Snout would nibble the magic mushrooms on the sly and spill the crab apple juice. He was also very bad at catching earwigs. Witch Wurzel needed an apprentice to prepare her spells properly. So, one morning, she set off in search of a child to help her.

At the foot of Bald Mountain there was a cottage where two cousins, Nicholas and Sarah, lived. They never went into the dark pine woods on the slopes of Bald Mountain, because of the bats that flitted about there and the owls that screeched.

This afternoon they were sitting by the well playing with Pattypaws, Nicholas's kitten. Nicholas always fed Pattypaws on special scraps he saved from his meals, and she followed him everywhere.

Witch Wurzel crept up to the hedge that grew around the well and peeped over the top.

"These children look a suitable size," she thought. "One of them will do nicely as an apprentice." Just then, Sarah's mother called her.

The girl reluctantly left her cousin playing with Pattypaws and went to join her mother. Witch Wurzel flicked hastily through her alphabetical book of magic to find the spell she wanted: "Fungus ... Frogspawn ... Aha, here we are, Forgetfulness."

She crawled out from behind the hedge and glared at Nicholas, who froze in terror.

Fumbling in her pockets, she brought out the magic ingredients and threw them at Nicholas's feet. Then she chanted the spell:

"*Adder's bite and dead dog's bone,*
Forget all you have ever known,
Aunties, uncles, cousins too,
And do what I shall ask of you."

120

Pattypaws had scurried into the bushes. Nicholas's face went blank and he stared helplessly at Witch Wurzel.

"That should do very well," she cackled gleefully. "Now follow me, child," and Nicholas did just that.

When Sarah returned she found Pattypaws mewing sadly, and there was no sign of Nicholas at all. She searched in the orchard and down by the river, but he was nowhere to be found. That night all the villagers went in seach of him, but not a trace could be found. And they were all too frightened of witches to look in the woods on Bald Mountain.

Meanwhile, Witch Wurzel was delighted with her new servant. Silent and obedient, he mixed her glasses of nasty toadslime, he diced the fungus and cleaned the filthy cauldron, all at her command. Snout was no longer needed, and he sulked by the broomsticks. Nicholas never asked about his home, because he had forgotten that he ever had one.

121

All day he worked making spells, and at night he slept by the glowing cauldron.

Sarah's mother and the villagers decided that Nicholas would never return. Perhaps he had been swept away by the river and drowned. But Sarah felt sure that he was still alive somewhere. One day she was out walking, when a big black crow landed on a branch above her.

"Big black crow," sighed Sarah. "Can you tell me where my cousin is?" To her amazement, the crow opened his big beak and spoke:

> *"In Wild Witch Wurzel's gloomy caves,*
> *Your cousin Nicholas toils and slaves.*
> *Follow the path up the mountain side,*
> *And there you will find where the Wild Witch hides!"*

Sarah started forward to ask the crow more questions, but he had already flapped away. So she made her way back to the cottages, and resolved that she would go in search of her cousin. The next morning she set off along the winding path which led through the pine trees and up to the top of Bald Mountain.

Witch Wurzel was in a very good mood that morning. Nicholas and Snout had mixed her a revolting spotty potion, which she was going to sprinkle on the village teacher. She was sitting outside her cave, picking her teeth with a bat's claw, when she caught sight of Sarah coming up the mountain side.

"Aha!" she cried. "That silly girl. Come to fetch her cousin, no doubt. Well, my forgetfulness spell has lasted good and strong. He'll never recognise her."

Sarah shivered when she caught sight of the huge cauldron and the sinister figure of Witch Wurzel.

122

Then Witch Wurzel called out to her.

"Step this way, child. After your cousin, aren't you? Well, you'll soon see how strong my magic is."

Sarah stepped nervously forward. Just at that moment, Nicholas came out of the cave carrying a huge bundle of firewood for the cauldron.

"Nicholas!" cried Sarah, and ran forward to hug him. But Nicholas stared at her blankly, as though he had never seen her before. Witch Wurzel cackled in delight.

"He can't remember a thing!" she crowed. "See how strong my magic is!"

"I'll make him remember," said Sarah bravely. "I'll find a way."

Witch Wurzel was enjoying herself. She decided to play a game with this cheeky child – a game the girl would be sure to lose.

"Very well," she sneered. "Just see if you can make him remember. If you can, you can have him. But you will not succeed."

Sarah went over to her cousin, who was working inside the cave. He was busy stirring the witch's steaming cauldron, cooking up another horrid-smelling spell. He didn't even look up when Sarah went over and laid her hand gently on his arm.

"Nicholas," she said desperately. "You must remember our cottage and the hens in the back yard." But Nicholas just glanced at her and went back to his work. Witch Wurzel roared with laughter. This was good fun! Sarah tried again.

"Remember the wooden squirrel you carved that hangs by your bed," she said. "And the grandfather clock that doesn't work." But still Nicholas just looked at her as though he did not understand. Witch Wurzel cackled in delight.

Then suddenly, there was a loud mewing. Sarah looked down in astonishment to see Pattypaws racing towards Nicholas. The kitten must have followed her all the way up the mountain! Instantly Nicholas stopped looking blank. He knelt down and picked up Pattypaws, who purred and licked his face. Then he jumped up and hugged his cousin. "Sarah!" he cried happily.

125

Witch Wurzel flew into a furious rage. She scowled and shrieked and tried to bundle Nicholas back into her cave. But Sarah stepped between them.

"You promised to let him go if he remembered," she cried. "Your spell has worn off! You promised!"

Witch Wurzel could not break her promise. She spluttered with anger as Sarah led her cousin and Pattypaws away down Bald Mountain and back home, but she could do nothing. When the villagers heard that a little kitten had managed to break one of the witch's wicked spells, they all stopped being afraid of her. As for Witch Wurzel, she was so ashamed that she flew away and was never seen again.

THE END

The Witches who Came to Stay

by Philip Steele

Once upon a time there were three wicked witches, who went to sea in a ship full of holes. The ship's mast was an upturned broomstick and, instead of a flag, there were tattered streamers of seaweed. As soon as the ship set sail, the sky turned yellow and filled with big black clouds. A storm came whirling across the bay, tossing the spray up into the wind. But the ship sped on and on, scudding over the waves like a cormorant. And if you had listened carefully above the howling wind, you might have heard the wicked witches singing to themselves:

> *"Sea snakes and jelly fish,*
> *Octopi and smelly fish,*
> *Skellingtons in wellingtons*
> *Forty fathoms deep!"*

The wicked witches cackled with glee, and then peered through their telescopes.

"Land ahoy! Land ahoy!"

The ship sped on and on, towards a little island on the horizon...

Granite Island was a lonely place, especially during an autumn storm. Fergus the Fisherman pulled his boat high up on the beach, and went home to his little stone cottage.

"What an evening!" he said to himself, as he barred the door behind him. "Why, it must be nearly Hallowe'en!" He put a big kettle on the fire, and pulled off his boots. Outside, the storm was raging. Waves were crashing against the sea wall. Fergus could hear them: Crash! Splash! Splosh!
It was at times like this that he wished he didn't live all on his own.

128

Just then, Fergus heard a knock on the door. Or was
it simply a loose plank banging in the wind? Was that
rain spattering on the window pane? Or maybe the
scrabble of long finger nails? And was that the sound of
the wind, or someone singing?

> *"Skellingtons in wellingtons*
> *Forty fathoms deep!..."*

Fergus shivered. Then he strode across to the door and
flung it open. In tumbled a bedraggled brood of witches,
who fell on the floor in a heap!

"Who the devil are you?" thundered Fergus.

A thin witch with knobbly knees untangled herself.
She pulled on her tall black hat, which was dripping wet.

"I am Bignose, a wicked witch," said she, "and I can
turn you into a sea slug – just like that!" She snapped her
bony fingers.

129

A big fat witch with fifteen double chins was the next to get up on her feet. She carried a large carpetbag.

"I am Fishface, an even wickeder witch!" said she, "and I can turn you into an archaeopteryx!"

Fergus didn't know what an archaeowhatsit was, but he didn't like the sound of it at all. Still, he put a brave face on it. He pulled up the third witch by her scarlet shawl.

"And which witch are you?" he demanded.

"Which witch? *Which witch?* Are you *mocking* me?" The third witch turned towards him, and she had the most beautiful face Fergus had ever seen. Her long red hair was a tangle of curls, and her eyes were as blue as the summer sea. "Because if you *are* mocking me," she went on, "I shall turn you into driftwood and burn you on the fire! My name is Belladonna, and I have come to stay here for Hallowe'en, with my aunties Fishface and Bignose!"

"Oh, you have, have you? And who invited you?" Fergus was furious, but all three witches stared at him sternly, and he had no desire to be frizzled and fried, or turned into some creepy-crawly. "All right, all right," he added quickly. "You can stay. But only for Hallowe'en mind you..."

"Agreed," snapped Bignose. "Now, we three are very tired, so we'll be off to bed."

"And in the meantime I suggest you prepare our breakfast for tomorrow," added Fishface.

Fergus cursed his luck. Witches to stay! They'd cause all sorts of trouble. And where was he to sleep? Here in the chair? Fishface and Bignose indeed! Belladonna was very beautiful, it was true ...but wasn't

it she who wanted to make firewood out of him? What was Fergus to do?

The night passed by, and Fergus dozed fitfully by the fire. The wind was still moaning around the cottage. As the firelight flickered, Fergus caught sight of a book sticking out of Fishface's carpetbag. He carefully pulled it out and looked at the cover. It was called *Every Witch's Handbook of Practical Spells*. He turned the pages with growing excitement.

After half an hour, Fergus pulled on his boots and slipped out of the front door. He returned around dawn, his pockets bulging with odds and ends which he emptied out on the table. There was a crab's claw and a dollop of tar, some clammy seaweed and a smelly old fish bone! What was he up to?

The next day the witches woke up to a delicious smell of cooking. Sunshine was pouring in through the door.

"Breakfast time, you wicked witches!" called Fergus. "Tasty pies to start the day!"

"Well, this *is* nice," said Bignose, and gobbled up her pie in two mouthfuls.

"Yum, yum," she said, smacking her lips greedily. "That was very tasty!"

"Maybe we won't turn you into a sea slug after all," croaked Fishface, and gobbled up hers.

"Not until after the holiday's over," explained Belladonna, and smiled icily as she bit into her pie.

Suddenly the witches looked a little pale. Bignose was growing a yellow beak, and squawking like a gull! Fishface was turning into a plump porpoise, before their very eyes!!

"Shoo! Shoo!" laughed Fergus. The gull flew out of the front door, and away over the sea. Fergus threw the porpoise over the sea wall, and away it swam. Belladonna was white with rage. She started muttering spells, but Fergus just stood there chuckling.

"What have you done, you oaf?" said Belladonna, stamping her foot.

"I have used your little book to make some magic potions," replied Fergus. "Now you can have a taste of your own medicine. Your wicked aunties have been turned into animals for a year and a day. That should teach them better manners!"

"But what about *me*?" wailed Belladonna.

"You have just swallowed a love potion, and will love me as long as you live!"

And so she had and so she did. In fact, Fergus and Belladonna were married the very next day. Fergus was never lonely again, and Belladonna and he were very much in love. Sometimes Belladonna still tried out new spells, but she never ever wanted to turn Fergus into firewood. And sometimes, when the autumn gales blew, they could see a little black boat with a broomstick mast bob over the horizon, and in the wind they could hear snatches of songs about skeletons under the sea. But Fishface and Bignose never came to stay again. They had learned their lesson well.

THE END

GRUMBLOG

by Jane Garrett

There was once a beautiful land which was terrorised by an evil witch. Her name was Grumblog and she could not bear anything that was peaceful, happy or beautiful. It made her boil over with rage. Her eyes would send out showers of red sparks and thick black smoke would pour from her ears. The people in the village near the forest where she lived were terrified. They thought a volcano was erupting.

Grumblog's forest was a dangerous place. People entering it in search of blackberries, or wild mushrooms, seldom reappeared. So, a ripple of fear spread through the village one morning when a really loud and dreadful volcano rage from Grumblog was followed by an eerie silence. All the birds stopped singing. Nothing moved, except the wind in the trees.

The witch had got extremely cross at the sight of a blackbird singing to a pair of courting squirrels. She hated anyone to be happy. Spitting with terrible rage, she stirred her cauldron savagely. Then, looking up at the cloud of evil-smelling steam, she hissed:

"Fur and feather, be no more.
Turn to stone by Grumblog's lore."

In that instant, the whole forest fell silent. The villagers were so scared, they packed up their things and fled across the hills.

In the forest, all the wild creatures had been turned into stone. Tiny statues of mice, rabbits and deer stood, with surprised looks on their faces, by the side of the path. When the sound of all the frightened people running away faded, all that could be heard was the wheezing of Grumblog, cackling over the success of her spell.

It did not take long, however, for Grumblog to discover that she had made a serious mistake. The forest was more beautiful than ever before. Flowers blossomed where the rabbits and deer used to graze. And everything was quiet and peaceful around the witch's dark and gloomy home, where she sat, thinking up new ways of making everyone miserable.

Grumblog flung down her book of spells in disgust.

"This is no good at all," she roared. "Bring me whirlwinds and thunderstorms, typhoons and tornados." And she kicked the sleeping cauldron with her boot.

But the storms she unleashed made the forest fresher, greener and lovelier than ever. And as she stumped through the deserted forest and the empty countryside, the cottage gardens with their bright flowers seemed to mock her. Grumblog went purple with rage. Black trails of smoke curled up over the treetops, as she marched back to her dark, damp home.

137

Plunging her broomstick into the cauldron, she
stirred the magic brew as hard as she could, and cursed
the flowers with the most fearful spell she knew:

*"Cottage gardens, hedgerow weeds,
Live up to your names in deeds."*

No one knows whether Grumblog actually intended
the spell to work out the way it did, but immediately all
the plants began to change.

Dandelions and tiger lilies turned into real lions
and tigers, snarling crossly at each other. Elephant
grasses grew greyer and fatter, until they became a herd
of real elephants. The monkeypuzzle tree dissolved
into a chattering colony of apes. Cows emerged from
cowslips, and snapdragons grew into real dragons that
set fire to the tree tops as they flapped overhead. Then
all the plant-animals started chasing each other. The
elephants stampeded through the cows, the lions and
tigers fought the dragons — it was chaos! Grumblog was
absolutely delighted.

138

The witch sat back and watched as the animals crashed through the wood, tearing up the grass, burning the leaves, and barking and snarling at each other. She roared with laughter as they fought, and croaked "Bravo!" as they knocked over bushes and fences, broke windows and generally made a terrible mess.

Then, Grumblog froze with fear, for she suddenly realised that the roar of the dandelions and the wild trumpeting of the elephant grasses were coming closer. The thudding of heavy feet and the crashing of branches got louder and louder — the plant-animals were heading straight for her!!

Grumblog dashed back to her hovel and managed to hide, just as a huge, angry herd of elephants, lions, tigers and dragons came smashing their way into her clearing, snapping her broomstick underfoot — and sending her precious magic cauldron flying.

From the moment that the evil-smelling liquid from the broken cauldron seeped into the ground, the forest began to change. Grumblog's wicked spell was broken! And not only that spell – but all the evil spells she had ever done. The stone birds and animals dotted about the forest came to life again, and carried on exactly as though nothing had happened. And the plant-animals changed back into their true form.

Suddenly, the villagers couldn't remember why they had left their beautiful valley. Filled with gladness, they packed their bags again for the journey home. But what they saw when they got there took their breath away. Their lovingly tended gardens lay in ruins and their favourite flowers were scattered across the countryside. It took them weeks to tidy up the mess.

As for Grumblog, no one ever discovered what became of her. Once her magic powers were destroyed, she vanished from the forest for ever, leaving the land in peace at last.

THE END

THE WITCH WHO DIDN'T HAVE A CAT

by Sue Seddon

There was once a witch called Smoragda who didn't have a cat. The Chief Witch wasn't very pleased about it, and commanded Smoragda to come and explain her lack of a cat in person. So Smoragda mounted her broomstick and flew to Castle Greydoom.

"Now look here, Smoragda," began the Chief Witch. "You must get yourself a cat. All witches have a cat. You can't be a witch without one."

"I don't want a cat," whined Smoragda.

"Stuff and nonsense! Why ever not?" snapped the Chief Witch.

Smoragda looked at her through her slanty green eyes and cracked her knobbly knuckles crossly.

"I don't like cats," she said.

"Not like cats! NOT LIKE CATS!" shrieked the

142

Chief Witch, her crumpled face quivering with rage. "We'll see about that! I shall send you a cat tomorrow. Do not try to get rid of it with spells. My magic is stronger than yours. Now go home."

The next morning Smoragda was woken by a dreadful, earsplitting yowl outside her window.

"The cat!" she thought, and went to the door. Opening it, she saw a small, black cat sitting on the step.

"Scram!" yelled Smoragda, and slammed the door. A few moments later she opened it again. The cat was still there, with his back to her.

"Shoooooo!" hissed Smoragda. The cat didn't even twitch his tail. Then very slowly he turned his head and fixed his great yellow eyes on Smoragda and yawned.

"B-b-b-broomsticks and buffaloes," growled Smoragda, "this is going to be difficult." And she banged the door shut again.

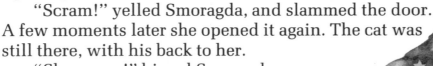
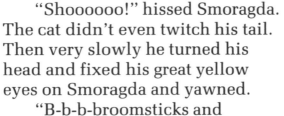
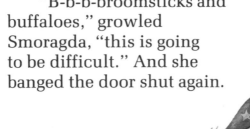

All that day Smoragda worked her way through her *Giant Book of Spells*, especially the 'Disappearing', 'Vanishing' and 'Getting Rid Of' sections. But the spells were all useless. At bedtime the cat was still on the doorstep, though he had curled up and gone to sleep.

"Drat this cat," said Smoragda. "If magic doesn't work, I shall have to take him somewhere and lose him! Now, where shall I take him?"

In the morning Smoragda opened the door and called the cat:

"Pussy, Pussy, Pussy! Who's a nice little Pussy then? Come to mummy."

The cat opened an eye and uncurled itself slowly. It looked down its nose at the witch's shaggy red hair and long green fingernails, then arched its back and had a good stretch. Smoragda grabbed it. It let out a fearful yowl, but she hung on and galloped towards her broomstick. After a terrible fight, Smoragda managed to tie the cat onto the handle of the broomstick and, leaping astride, she took off.

THE WITCH WHO DIDN'T HAVE A CAT

145

High into the sky they flew, higher than a plane, and faster than a train. The air screamed past them and flattened the cat's ears to its head and its whiskers to its cheeks. Smoragda untied the cat:

"Hang on pussy cat," she cried, "or you might just fall off." And she let out a dreadful shriek of laughter.

Now Smoragda was famous for her aerobatics. She had won prizes for looping the loop, and her sky dives were spectacular. Roaring through the sky with the cat behind her,

she threw her broomstick into all the high-flying tricks she knew. She zig-zagged, she curled, she dodged and stalled. She went into a record head-dive which made even her own stomach turn over – but she couldn't shake the cat off. He sat calmly through it all.

At last, in desperation, she looped the biggest loop. It was so enormous that her heels hit the stars and made sparks fly. Everyone on Earth saw hundreds of shooting stars.

"This is it, cat. Say goodbye!" yelled Smoragda, as broomstick, witch and cat fell from the top of the loop into a death-defying dive. Even Smoragda was using all her magic to stay on. Her pointed witches' hat disappeared and so did the cat. Smoragda looked back to make quite sure and shouted a triumphant "Hooray!" But, when she turned round again, what a shock she got! For there was the cat, sitting on the front of the broomstick enjoying every minute of it. He had climbed round to get a better view.

147

So they shot down to Earth together and Smoragda tried everything she knew to make the cat fall off. She dived into the deepest ocean, but the cat loved the fish and asked her to do it again. She travelled through the hottest deserts, but the cat loved the sun. She tried to freeze him in Antarctica, but he got on very well with penguins. She even took him to the moon, but he said he'd always wanted to be the first cat to land there.

Exhausted, Smoragda returned home. The cat smiled and asked when they could go up again.

Smoragda went to see the Chief Witch.

"Okay, you win!" she said. "I'll keep the cat. I'm beginning to think he's rather special."

"He is," answered the Chief Witch. "I gave him nine lives."

So that is how Smoragda the witch got her cat.

THE END

RACHEL
AND THE
MAGIC STONE

by Deborah Tyler

Rachel Green lived in the middle of a row of three cottages at the end of Orchard Lane. Her parents' house was a pretty little cottage, but the other two were very strange indeed. They were very ugly and very squat. They had lots of rickety black chimney pots and they were covered with strange carvings. The carvings were of fierce beasts and they seemed to roar at passersby. So you can see that the cottages were very strange indeed, and the reason they were so odd is because they belonged to two witches.

Rachel hated living there. It was no fun living between two old witches. Especially two old witches who were always arguing.

The two witches were sisters. Their names were Snatch and Grab and they were very mean. Snatch was

149

long and thin. She looked as if she was made out of sticks and joined together badly at the knees. She had a sharp nose, beady black eyes and no chin. She always wore purple lipstick and a pair of big emerald ear-rings. Sometimes, she wore an enormous hat, with flowers sticking out of it. It was really rather a funny hat, but no one dared to laugh at it.

Grab was as plain as her sister was colourful. Rachel always thought she looked as if she was made from a potato. She wore a grey jumper, a black skirt and thick, grey stockings, which always had huge holes in them. She had a fat, dimpled face and wild, wiry grey hair.

Long ago, the Great White Witch had given the two sisters a stone. It was a magic stone, made from unicorn's horn and dragon's wing, and it had very special powers. It could heal anything and it could also be used to cast spells.

In the summer, the magic stone shimmered a beautiful blue, like the sea. In the winter, it glowed like pure gold. The two sisters refused to share it. Each one wanted the stone for herself, and they argued all the time about who should have it. When Rachel's parents moved in between the two witches, they found themselves in the middle of a great argument.

Rachel was fed up with it. When the two witches were at their most angry, they made it rain. It had been raining now for two years.

And that wasn't all. Snatch and Grab shouted at each other through magic telephones made of giant sheep horns. They made smelly potions to upset each other, but these usually upset Rachel's mum more, especially when she wanted to hang the washing out. Sometimes they threw bolts of lightning at each other, which missed and landed in Rachel's back garden. In fact, Snatch and Grab were so busy arguing that they had forgotten all about the stone.

One day, in between rain storms, Rachel's mum and dad were sitting in the back garden and Rachel was playing in the front garden. Suddenly, she noticed something as bright as a pool of water, lying by the gate. It was the magic stone, and it was lovely! It shimmered as deep and as blue as a lake – and as Rachel looked at it, it spoke.

"They dropped me," said the stone, grumpily. "Can you believe that, eh?"

Rachel shook her head. The stone continued.

"They argue about me for years and years. Then they drop me and they don't even know that I'm gone. What a cheek!" It shone a bright leaf-green. "And think of all the trouble they have caused trying to get me – making bolts of fire, cooking up smells." The stone sighed. So did Rachel.

"They are rude," she said. "We should teach them a lesson."

"I don't think I can," the stone said in a sad voice. "What they don't realise is that they've used up nearly all my magic with their greedy quarrelling. I once belonged to a king of Egypt who wore me in his crown. Then I belonged to a mermaid who gave me to a brave and

153

handsome pirate. I am a very special magic stone. To think about the way all my power is being wasted by two silly old witches would break my heart, if I had one. The trouble is, if I stopped them now I would have no power left. All I would be is just a pretty stone.''

As the stone said this, there was a terrific boom in the back garden. Rachel looked round and was just in time to see a huge cloud of yellow smoke rising up behind the house. She also saw a pair of long legs disappear over the top of the hedge into Snatch's garden. Rachel dashed through the house. When she reached the back garden she was horrified. On the two deck chairs, where her mother and father had been sitting, there were two huge plants. Snatch had tried to turn Grab into a giant plant, but the spell had gone wrong. She had turned Rachel's parents into plants, instead!

154

Rachel ran back to the stone and explained what had happened.

"You have to help me now," she cried.

"All right," said the stone. "I don't know that I want to be magic any more, anyway. It was fun when I belonged to the king of Egypt, but being used by silly witches to turn sensible people's parents into plants is quite another matter."

The stone began to glow, then it flashed until orange sparks flew. Then the stone hummed. It recited a spell very grandly, and the whole back garden shook.

"Keep no spells," declared the stone. "Let them be witches no more." There was a flash of light, a loud bang and the stone turned blue again.

Rachel could hear her parents chattering to one another in their deck chairs. She sighed with relief. But what of Snatch and Grab? Just as she was wondering what had become of them, Rachel saw the most remarkable thing. Grab came out of her house and walked toward Snatch, who had appeared at just the same time.

"How nice to see you," said Grab.

"How lovely to see you," replied Snatch.

"Do come in and have some tea, my dear," said Grab, and they both walked back into the house.

"I have your stone," Rachel called to them.

"Stone? What stone?" they both asked.

Rachel held up the stone, which was now a dull blue.

"Oh, that!" said the sisters, together. "Keep it!"

So Rachel kept the stone. It was no longer magic. It was no longer anything but a pretty stone. Snatch and Grab were no longer bad witches. Their argument was over and it never rained on Rachel's house again.

When Rachel was older she had the stone made into a brooch and always wore it on special occasions. It shone a beautiful blue in summer, and a rich gold in winter, and Rachel liked it better than all her other jewels. For it reminded her of how stupid arguments can be and, after all, who else has a brooch made of unicorn's horn and dragon's wing? Or, for that matter, one that once belonged to a pirate, an Egyptian king and two silly witches?

THE END